THE PERFECT PAIRING

The Trouble with Mollie - Book Two

RAFFAELLA ROWELL

Published by Blushing Books
An Imprint of
ABCD Graphics and Design, Inc.
A Virginia Corporation
977 Seminole Trail #233
Charlottesville, VA 22901

Rafaella Rowell
The Perfect Pairing

eBook ISBN: 978-1-64563-764-6
Print ISBN: 978-1-64563-765-3
Audio ISBN: 978-1-64563-766-0
v2

Cover Art by ABCD Graphics & Design
This book contains fantasy themes appropriate for mature readers only. Nothing in this book should be interpreted as Blushing Books' or the author's advocating any non-consensual sexual activity.

Chapter 1

K athryn Ellis had focused non-stop on a project. She had worked with great energy with her friend, Mollie, to achieve results. They were setting down the last touches to a brand new dating app.

The system could select a 'top pick' amongst candidates based on matching criteria, giving it a score. The higher the score, the better a match. The features to match were many, such as core values, personality and character traits, interests, education and many more aspects of life, to predict a romantic desire and suggest people who could be kindred spirits for that purpose. They had driven this project for months since their return from France.

An old whim of theirs, they had put this off for a while, but now it absorbed all their spare time. Their hope was to achieve a notable success with the perfect pairing, by matching the right individuals for a loving relationship.

Following the perilous days in Antibes, they had wanted a task to absorb them, to forget the events that had almost shattered their lives. So the new app was the enterprise they needed to occupy themselves, to help them forgive and forget. They had thrown themselves wholeheartedly into it, dividing their time actively between their studies and this project.

They had used core coding and programming languages to build the app, customized features and functionalities to make it user friendly. Mollie had devised the algorithms behind its matching capabilities, but with all the components of data feeds now loaded, they were on the finishing line.

She looked up from her laptop. "God, I'll be happy when this project is done!" Mollie hissed with a small grin.

They sat in a coffee shop, a stone's throw away from the university's halls where they attended their classes, and they kept on bashing diligently at their keyboards while sipping their cappuccinos.

"I think we've cracked it; it should work," Kathryn said. "All we need now is a constant flow of live data to bring it to life, actual people profiles for the testing stage. I have already listed over one hundred fifty profiles of men and women who are keen to take part. I've told them this is only the test stage, but they agreed. All of them are singles, one or two frisky ones, the usual culprits, but we must make sure the app performs well, that it works. This is key," she added, taking another swig of coffee.

"I've placed an ad in the university newspaper too, to gain more profiles. We should get hundreds of people to take part. With March mid-term-break coming up in two weeks, we can run the trial after the holidays, to aim for a launch in July. Three months of testing should do it," Mollie replied, read-justing her chair at the table, having another sip of her cappuccino.

It was early-March in Oxford, and the winter in England so far had been rather mild for that time of the year, so she took off her scarf. She was getting hot in the jam-packed coffee shop.

"People will be able to download the app and enroll themselves in it once it's live in July. And they'll get their match, their potential partner for life. Perhaps even their soulmate! The perfect pair! Great, ha?" Kathryn smiled. "They'll view the profile of the 'top pick' candidate and decide if they wish to proceed to date them," she went on, "though it would be wonderful to make some money out of this, too, if we can. I know you don't need it, Mollie, with a wealthy husband like Zac Sorensen, but I would welcome it. This town is so expensive." She trailed off, fantasizing great achievements, fame and fortune.

"It'll be a success. You just wait," Mollie replied, dismissing her friend's worries with a wave of her hand.

"Hey, I forgot to tell you. Even Marguerite wants to take part."

"Marguerite?"

"Yes. The French girl in the senior post-graduate admin office, the one around the corner from Corpus Christi. Surely, you know her. She is so efficient. When I have a bother with fees, papers, exams or whatever it is, she sorts everything out for me, before I even have time to speak. I like her; she is awesome."

"Oh, yes. They call her Margot, don't they? Of course. She is so pretty, but by God, sometimes she can be so serious. The poor girl hardly ever smiles. I don't think she has even accepted one date yet, so far. All the boys have tried to date her, with no success. I wonder why she has chosen our app, though. She always declines every man."

"Yes, I was surprised, too. Who knows? But she is so sweet when you get to know her," Kathryn said. "We'll see who comes up as her 'top pick,' then?"

"Guess what, Kat, and please don't get mad at me, but I have entered your profile, too, and you match up perfectly to

Fin, to ninety percent, no less," Mollie said with a satisfied smile.

Her companion stared at her, astonished. "What? You did what?" Kathryn replied, flabbergasted when she recovered, while her head went back a touch and her eyes became wide with incredulity.

"Aha!"

"No!"

"Oh, yes."

"I can't believe it. Fin…to me?"

"Completely. The app says so."

"Wait a minute. Did he offer you his profile to enter?" she asked, narrowing her eyes on Mollie.

"Umm… no. But I know him well enough, and I discreetly questioned Zac about him, too."

"So, Fin didn't allow you to use his data, then."

"Well… no, not in so many words… I mean, not yet…"

"Oh, Mollie, you are impossible. You have no permission."

"Kat, stop fussing. We're only in the testing phase. I'll delete his information when we go live. Anyway, ninety percent, and you match! To Finley, no less! Forget the damn permission. What do you say to that? Compatible, you and him, brilliant. Ha!"

"It can't be! Finley, my 'top pick'? Are you sure? Oh, dear…"

"Oh, stop whining. He is your perfect pairing. I know we haven't tested the damn app yet, but, girl, you cannot get a score much higher than that."

"No. Impossible! And you had no right to do this."

"Oh, for God's sake, Kat! I tell you, yes, he is. Stop talking, and here, come and have a look."

They put their heads together, the brunette and the redhead, looking at the screen on Mollie's laptop. Kathryn's chestnut eyes became enormous as she read the results. She shook her head, not believing what she was seeing. She was shocked. Dismayed, she put a hand over her mouth. She was speechless!

"I don't think so," Kathryn muttered under her breath, as the shock subsided, with more vigorous shakes of her head as she read the conclusions on the app. "It can't be!" she inhaled. "No way!" She pursed her lips for a moment, thinking. "Then, for certain, we need to do more work on this app!" Kathryn continued with a grimace. "I doubt it's correct!" She sighed, frustrated, "You know, Fin and I have only had three dates since we came back from Antibes. That's all, in eight months! Can you imagine that? Eight months… three dates! How do you explain that, then? So, I suspect the damn app is not right, after all this work. Oh, God! I don't even think Finley likes me. The man is frustrating," Kathryn summed up with a deep sigh.

"Fin likes you—a lot! And you know it, so stop fussing. I could predict this even without the damn app, I tell you. But he is always busy. My husband and Fin work hard. You must have realized that by now. And consider yourself lucky, at least, you and Finley are in the same town. Poor Clarissa saw Alex once in eight months. The man is always preparing something, or rather, involved in some major national case in the litigation courts," Mollie explained.

"Is he? Poor Clarissa."

"Yes, poor girl. She has given up on him. I mean, she lives in Babbacombe, in Devon, near Mother's, and Alex is in London, four hours' drive apart. Theirs is impossible. So I think Claris has thrown in the towel. At least, you see Fin every evening at my house. I told you these men are busy, work-horses, work phenomenon. I have not seen my husband for the last three days, he's been so busy, other than for a good morning kiss." Mollie's lips formed in a thin line, thinking how much she had missed Zac.

The problem was Mollie's husband, Zac Sorensen, and his friends were workaholics.

During the dreadful events in Antibes eight months ago, Peter had fired two bullets on him which had broken his collarbone and shattered his forearm. The wounds made him undergo several operations during the past months. It had not been easy for them.

He was healing, and when the cast finally came off his arm, Zac had thrown himself even harder back into his work to catch up for the lost time.

His security firm kept on growing, protecting the rich and famous, working with top sporting and music events, too. It was a great success. So, her husband and his buddy were always busy.

Finley Harman, an ex-soldier in the army, was his best friend and partner in the company, and Kathryn liked him a lot. She had taken an instant liking to him all those months ago.

The partnership in the firm came in readiness for the time Zac would move full time to head his family business as its CEO, while Finley would take over the security company. As a result, they were two men who were hard to pin down, working long hours, always busy.

Mollie thought this could only get worse when her husband eventually succeeded his father on the board of their multibillion family real estate and hotel enterprise. But she could not help that. Mollie would have to accept it, though she loved Zac dearly.

"Why don't you come home for dinner tonight. I'm sure Zac will turn up with Fin as usual. He is always at my house, so you can see him then," Mollie said to her friend.

"Oh, thank you, maybe. But you're right, if I'm not there with you, I don't see him at all," Kathryn sighed, but her companion snorted.

"Well, you and he spend so much time at my house, that's why he doesn't ask you out. He can meet you there whenever he wants. I think he is a cheapskate. Why invest money on a date with you when he can see you at my house for free?"

"Ooh, Mollie, that's not it at all, it's not fair, and you know it. Fin is generous. He always buys things for us. The problem is the man can't make up his mind about me. That's what! Oh, God! I wish he would decide whether he likes me or not. I am getting impatient with him. If he thinks I'll wait forever, he has another think coming."

"Oh, come home, Kat. It'll be fun. But he loves you, I am certain. And the app is not wrong. He only has eyes for you; you can't miss that. Surely, you know this by now. Go on; come for dinner."

"Fine. I will. I am entering Ethan's data too, in the app, I mean. He has agreed to take part."

"Oh? I am sure that boy gets taller by the minute, the tallest student in Physics. Hell, no, in the entire university. No, I tell a lie, in the entire city of Oxford! Bloody hell, the guy is tall." Mollie chuckled.

"Oh, stop it. It would be good to see if Ethan has any affinities to me," Kathryn said, launching a playful glance at her friend, "You know, Fin has not kissed me... not even once."

"I thought you had three dates with him?"

"Yes, but he has not kissed me yet, not once. I guess he doesn't like me that way. Let me tell you, our app is wrong. You are mistaken, Mollie. If he did, Fin would have done something about it after eight months, don't you agree? I mean, I know when we are in your house, we get on so well, we have fun, he's lovely. I can sense he likes me then, but he has never said a word to me. Maybe he just wants to be friends. He likes me as a friend, nothing more."

"Has Ethan said something to you? Is that it? Is this the reason you feel so doubtful about Finley tonight?"

"Well, no, I mean… um… Ethan asked me out for a drink tonight. That's all. But I said I'd think about it. Oh, Mollie, I can't wait forever for Fin to make a move on me, can I? As much as I adore him… What if he doesn't want me that way? What can I do?"

"Nonsense. Fin adores you," Mollie replied, but she narrowed her eyes and was pensive for a while. "Umm… I just had an idea," she went on, "say yes to Ethan; go out with him. We'll tell Fin you are dating, see if that moves his ass into gear. If it doesn't, then we have more work to do on the damn app. Though I suspect he'll move fast, once he knows you are dating. He is your perfect mate, your perfect pairing. It is in black and white, ninety percent, girl! We can't be mistaken after all that hard work. Our app says so."

"You see, you are doubting it too now, aren't you?"

"Rubbish! Fin is your match, the 'top pic' for you. Yes, do it. Go on a date with Ethan. I'll ask Zac to bring his friend home for supper, and he'll get a hell of a surprise, too." Mollie laughed.

"Tonight? Oh, I'm not sure that's a good idea. What if Fin gets upset? Ha?"

"What the hell, he needs a push, so we will give the man a push, simple."

"Do you think it'll work?" Kathryn asked.

"Well, if it doesn't, at least you'll know for sure. Call Ethan; do it. Meet him for a drink."

"Ooh, I don't know. I am nervous about it. I don't wish to upset Fin, or Ethan, for that matter. What if it backfires on me?"

"Bloody hell, Kat, do you want to know if the man likes you or not? Then do it. Go out with Ethan. Fin will be jealous if he likes you, and I am sure he does. You'll see; trust me. We are only going to give him an extra push." Mollie giggled.

"Oh, God, what have I got to lose? It's just a drink," Kathryn said, inhaling and closing her eyes.

She dialed Ethan's number on her mobile with a timid grin. Anything to hurry Finley along was a brilliant idea to her. Kathryn adored the bear of a man, but he was always the perfect gentleman with her, to her great chagrin. She had fantasies of love about him. She even had a few sexy dreams about him, to her own dismay.

"Hi, Ethan, Kat here. Do you still want to take me out for that drink tonight?" She hesitated, waiting for the answer at the other end of the phone, blushing furiously, hoping the young lad hadn't change his mind. "Good, I'll see you at 9:30 pm," she went on with a small satisfied smirk. "Perfect, meet you there."

"I'll tell you what we'll do. Let's go home, and you stay for dinner until it's time to meet with Ethan, and then you say goodbye to us. And to Fin, of course! Fabulous. So he can see you leave for a date with a man, all dolled up. Brilliant! I'll transform you into a sexy siren for your amorous date tonight. Fin will be speechless and jealous when he sees you. You'll look divine. Wait until I am done with you." Mollie clapped her hands in excitement at her master plan.

Kathryn Ellis was a student at Oxford University. She was doing a master's in physics, and she was not even twenty-two years old yet, a delightful and clever young girl.

Some people would say she was rather plain, including herself, but when you observed her, she was an enchanting girl. Lovable, a graceful brunette, with a sinuous, curvy, rather shapely fuller figure; incidentally, the type of figure Finley liked so much. Her bosom tended towards a large size, but she was proud of this feature, a little less on her hips, though.

Her huge, warm, almond-shaped eyes were extraordinary, the color of chestnuts, with long eyelashes framing them. Those eyes rendered her lovely. Her long, dark hair was luscious and complemented her features well, making her an attractive girl. Feminine was the word most men used for her.

Above all, she was enchanting, with a mellow and sunny personality, but with a streak of dogged determination which ran deep within her, showing itself off at the most unlikely of moments.

Her friends were devoted to her. Though, sometimes, she would say something embarrassing, putting her foot in her mouth. She was renowned for her blunders. But the world was her oyster. Mollie was her best friend and a fellow student.

Though Kathryn's love for Finley was the thorn in her side, he was the only man who mattered to her. She had first set eyes on him at Mollie's wedding. He had been Zac's best man. They had enjoyed a few dances together and had a wonderful time, but it was not until she saw him again, a week later in Antibes, that she fell in love with him.

Following her revelations of Peter's treachery and his subsequent violence, which left her battered, with black and blue bruises and stitches, Finley had stayed at her bedside in the hospital all night, taking care of her. He had soothed her with affection after her ordeal, making her feel safe again.

Thus, she had fallen in love with Finley and pined for him ever since. But the fellow didn't seem to make up his mind. Since her return from Antibes eight months ago, they had seen each other almost every night in Mollie's house, but the man had shown no romantic interest towards her, despite three dates. Or was it, perhaps, because of them? She didn't know. Finley had not even kissed her on any of those dates.

She was at her wits' end.

But there were times he was so lovable and captivating with her that she couldn't understand why he would not take her out on a date or declare his love to her. So, she wasn't sure where she stood with him. If she wanted to see him, Mollie's house was the place.

He spent an awful lot of time working with Zac after office hours, too, at his home, and most days, he dined there too. So, Kathryn became even more than a habitué at Mollie and Zac's, to stay close to Finley.

Chapter 2

They were now in the garden room in Mollie's home. It was chilly at this time of the year, but they liked the serenity of it. They were still working on their laptops, while waiting for the men for supper.

Mollie had given Kathryn a makeover for her date with Ethan, making her look and feel divine.

"I am entering Lord Buckley's data," Kathryn said.

"Lord Buckley?"

"I mean his son's information. I did a two-month internship at his firm recently, remember? I got close to the old fog. He is rather sweet when you get to know him. He is nice to young interns."

"Oh, he is a dear, I get along with him so well. He is ill, you know, the poor man. Though he has his good and bad days. We should visit him to see how he is. He is one of Zac's clients and his father's friend; they are old friends. He gave a party in January, and he told me about you working for him, and that you had a chat on this. Lord Buckley asked a lot of questions on our app—its capabilities, the chances of a suitable match, percentages, and all that staff," Mollie said.

"His son is an ogre, though. I am sure he is. Have you seen him? Oh, don't get me wrong, I don't mean physically. He is a good-looking man, no doubt. I mean the fellow is tall, lean, gorgeous, but by God, he has the personality of an ogre. Everyone in the office feared him. Hell, I think everyone in the world fears the young Lord." Kathryn hesitated then continued, "I tell you, Lord Buckley called me out of the blue two weeks ago and offered me a huge amount of information on his son to input on our app. He was ranting; it's his son's duty to the title to get heirs and all that."

"The young man gave you his permission to enter his data, did he?" Mollie scoffed and raised an eyebrow at her friend.

"This is a test—" she replied, blushing.

"So, who's got no permission now, hey?"

"The old fog mentioned he would get permission from his son to do this."

"Will he? Umm…"

"Fergus, his son—they call him Gus—I have seen him a few times in the office. They warned me to stay clear of him. You know, he never, ever smiled at me, not once. I am not surprised. For a good-looking chap, and young, the fellow is ill-tempered, cantankerous, a despot! Oh, he is handsome, though, so gorgeous, I think he might be even better looking than Zac—" Kathryn added, glimpsing at her companion with a wink, but she didn't get the chance to finish.

"*My husband is the loveliest of mortals,* I'll have you know! The most handsome of all!" Mollie stated primly, quoting the Greek poet, Homer, which in her mind, always described her husband to perfection.

Her friend snorted. "Maybe so! But that Gus fellow—'his great lordship' as some of the guys in the office call him—good heavens, the man is handsome too, you must admit. But as grumpy as a bear first thing in the morning. Let me see, how old is he?" Kathryn said, pressed some keys on her laptop.

"Thirty-three years old. Umm, I thought he was younger than that, but no, he is thirty-three."

"He was at Eton and Oxford at the same time as Zac. They are old friends, not sure how close they are. Handsome, you are right, but scary. The man frightens me, handsome and danger- ous. We'll have a hell of a job to match him to a woman. I'll be surprised if he accepted to take part in this at all, I understand he doesn't want to marry," Mollie replied.

"Ah, well, you are probably right, to be honest. But the old man begged me. He wanted to see if there was a girl who would match up to his son. Though he doubted that there was anyone prepared to take him on. But that's all he wants to know." Kathryn laughed. "I have the suspicion the old fellow will trick him into this somehow. Old Buckley is clever, you know, and he always gets his way."

"Bloody hell. I hope the old man knows what he is doing. But when we match him to someone, the poor creature will need a prize to handle this grumpy young man-bear. I don't think I've ever seen him smile, either. Does he match to anyone?"

"Don't know, haven't finished yet," Kathryn replied.

But they were interrupted. The housekeeper hovered in the doorframe, and Mollie looked up from her laptop. "Come in," Mollie said, and the woman made her way into the room.

"Mrs. Sorensen, when would you like dinner served? It is ready when you are. Your husband has just arrived."

"Thank you, Mrs. Johnson," Mollie said. "Zac, darling!" She rose upon seeing her husband, giving him the sunniest smile she possessed as he entered the room with his friend, then she turned to his companion. "Finley…" she perked up as she threw Kathryn, who blushed furiously, a knowing look.

"Ladies!" Both men said their hellos, but Zac gave his wife a loving kiss.

Finley's eyes grew enormous at Kathryn as he noticed her

big, beautifully styled hair and flawless makeup. She was all dressed up, too. He looked her up and down, from head to toe, seeing her all dolled up in a short mini-skirt, sexy boots and a white, sequined camisole that took his breath away, showing off her voluptuous bosom to perfection. His eyes caressed her, and doing the welcoming for him, his usual slight smile of appreciation spread wider across his face.

Kathryn blushed at his obvious inspection and delight of her. *I hope he doesn't think I've done this for him; he'll be rather disappointed, umm.*

She was beginning to get cold feet, though he said nothing to her.

"Are you boys hungry? Dinner is ready when you are. We are starving," Mollie stated.

"You go to the dining room; we'll be there in five," Zac urged.

"That's your answer, Mrs. Johnson. Let's have supper in about ten minutes," she told the housekeeper.

———

Mollie Belloc had married Zac Sorensen over eight months ago. He was the golden bachelor then, a wealthy man who owned his own security firm. In addition, his father had raised him to take over the family business, too, as CEO, a multi-billion-pound corporation, when he retired.

The Board of Directors had opposed Zac taking over the company. They thought his lifestyle was not suitable for such a powerful role. He was a playboy, and he didn't want to settle down. So, Zac had wed Mollie in a marriage of convenience. The relationship had started as a business arrangement to appease the board on his womanizing conduct.

Though, they had not counted on falling in love. Furthermore, in Antibes, Zac had discovered it had been Peter, his treacherous friend and Mollie's ex-boyfriend, who had come up with the elaborate plan for her to marry him for money, shaking the relationship to the core when the truth came out. Though no one had known until then, the scheming man, Peter, had a much darker plan in mind for his friend. Eventually, it all unraveled in a showdown, when Zac almost lost his life, culminating in Peter's demise. The events had shaken them to the core.

So, despite the lies and rocky start to their marriage, they had conquered their differences, and the young lovers had stayed together, shifting the relationship into a sincere and loving one.

Mollie adored Zac, and he worshipped her, but both could be stubborn. They were still getting to know one another, sometimes plundering their way through marriage. But they were in love.

"Oh, there you are. We were about to start without you. We're famished," Mollie told them. The girls were at the table with drinks, waiting when the men appeared.

"Mrs. Johnson, please, go ahead," Zac said to the housekeeper, so they began the evening meal.

"Zac, I hope you won't lock yourself in your study tonight after supper, or I'll be all alone," Mollie stated at one point during dinner. She turned a knowing glimpse to her companion, who dropped her eyes and fidgeted with her fork.

"Alone? Why?" Zac asked, darting a glance at Kathryn, who frequently remained until late in the house, and often she even stayed the night.

Finley looked up from his plate where he was tucking into a wonderful mustard-crusted lamb-rib with sour cream on the side, red potatoes and spinach, which had made his mouth water, while his nostrils had delighted in the bold, pungent English yellow mustard aroma, but little did he know what was about to happen. He stared at her.

"Yes, Kathryn has to leave in about fifteen minutes," Mollie replied.

"Why? Do you have an early class tomorrow?" Finley asked her with a tender smile.

It was true; he had never kissed the girl, and three dates had not been enough for him, but he enjoyed her company every night there. The two of them were always in Zac's house, Finley, as Zac's long-standing friend and business partner now in the security firm, and Kathryn, as Mollie's friend and fellow student.

Finley felt cozier with Kathryn there than on any date. It seemed homey to him, and he cherished her. He sensed the girl was true to herself there, without the artificiality of a date. He loved her eyes, the first thing he'd spotted when they met, and when those eyes glanced at him with the loveliest sparkle he had ever seen, his soul warmed, and his cock stirred.

But she was young, barely twenty-two-years-old, while he was over eleven years her senior. So, Finley wished to be certain the girl felt the same way about him as he felt about her, that it was not an infatuation for her, a fleeting, passing moment. He was guarded. He had promised himself that before he made a resolute move on her, he wanted to make sure of her affections for him.

He liked to take his time with his women, with the ones he wanted. He didn't like to rush things, in particular when the girl was so young. But he admired Kathryn, more than a lot. If truth be told, he adored the spirited girl. He had bonded with her instantly, when he first met her at Zac's wedding. A week later, in Antibes, he developed feelings of protectiveness and affection towards her. And within a few days, these feelings for her had deepened and turned into love instead.

He realized she was 'the girl'. No matter what, he decided pigheadedly, she was the woman for him, and she was his. Eight months later, he was more convinced than ever. He had a hunch she loved him too, but he needed to be sure. She was too young and inexperienced.

"Do you have an early class tomorrow?" Finley repeated, when she didn't answer the first time.

Kathryn shook her head, burned crimson and dropped her eyes, sipping her red wine. Still, she gave him no reply. She was about to lose her nerve if he kept asking.

"No. She has a date," Mollie said coolly and emptied her drink, struggling to avert eye contact with the men.

Finley's fork rattled on his plate, and his eyes drifted into slits, staring at Kathryn sitting opposite him, who drew a good swig of her wine while peering through the glass at his thunderous face.

A shocked silence descended for a few moments until Kathryn coughed at his accusing glance and cleared her throat.

Zac looked from Finley, to the girl, to Mollie, who kept the coolest, most innocent smile on her face, as if she had never concocted the plan.

"A date? With a man?" Finley thundered after a few seconds, and Kathryn gulped.

She finished the wine in her glass in one go.

"Yes, Fin, my friend has a date with a man," Mollie scoffed. "You recall the tall student of physics who's come here a few times to study with us, don't you, Zac? Well, he's asked Kat out. It is about time she went on a date," she said primly with a side glimpse at Finley, while her husband looked confused.

Finley looked at the girls, each one in turn. He studied them for a moment. He had the suspicion he was being played like a schoolboy.

"Well, excuse me. I-I must go, or I-I'll be late. Thank you

for dinner, darling," Kathryn stammered to her friend, though she faltered for a second. "See you tomorrow. Nice to see you, Zac and... ahem... F-Fin. Bye." And she dashed along from the room before she lost her nerve.

"I'll show you out." Mollie followed, catching her husband's sudden displeasure to her.

At the entrance hall, the girls chuckled. The first part of their plan had worked well.

"Did you hear his stern voice, look at his face? He didn't like it. What did I tell you? Fin loves you," Mollie stated with an amused grin. "He sounded upset."

"Upset? He's had months to ask me out. He has no right to be troubled now. Three dates are not much, are they? I've been waiting for ages, here, in your home every night, on the off chance he would say something to me, to see him. But nothing, not a word. Fin is not my boyfriend, nor has he made any advances on me. He has not said a romantic word to me, not for love nor money. For God's sake, we haven't even kissed, not a peck on the cheek. Yes, he is rather abrupt with women, I know, but by God, I can't wait forever until he decides whether or not he likes me. Don't you think eight months is a long time to decide if you like someone?" Kathryn said in a scowl, wide-eyed, her large doe-eyed chestnuts for once showing annoyance.

She flicked her long dark hair back over the shoulder, raising her feminine chin, ready to defy him if necessary. *Will he do something? Not that he would dare,* she had no doubt! *The fellow is cold,* and she was squandering her time with him, she reflected, exasperated. The trouble was she could not help loving the man, adoring him like a follower adores her God!

She rose on her toes for a moment, in rebellion at her own feelings.

At five feet four inches tall, she was shorter than Mollie, but Kathryn had a sinuous womanly figure compared to her companion's willowy frame. A figure that delighted Finley every time he set eyes on her.

"Yes, darling! You go and enjoy your date. I'll tell you in the morning what Fin said. That's assuming he says or does anything, but if he doesn't, then I suggest you keep dating Ethan, or someone else, and forget all about Fin."

"What's the point? He might not have liked it and yet, he said nothing, not a word other than 'A date? With a man?' I am astonished. I am furious now. Does he think he owns me? Why shouldn't I have a date, ha? He is just stringing me along. He was so shocked as if... as if I couldn't get a date with a man. Am I that ugly? I know I am rather plain, and he is handsome and can get any girl he wants, but is this what he assumes, that I cannot get a date with a man? Well, I have news for him! Who the devil does he think he is? Just because he is gorgeous, tall, hot and... well, I'll show him! See if I care."

"Umm, you do have it badly, don't you? You like him! Ha!" Mollie scoffed. But Kathryn silenced her with a frustrated look, and her companion steadied her features again, with her lips in a thin line, trying not to laugh.

"I'd better go, or I'll be late for my date, and yes, with a man! Bye, darling, see you tomorrow," she muttered, kissed her companion's cheeks, spun on her heels and left.

Finley Harman came from a humble background. He was the son of the driver in the old Sorensen household, and the boys had grown up together as children, known each other forever, and were longstanding friends, despite the differences in backgrounds and upbringing.

When Zac's wealthy grandfather died, he'd left his companion a small legacy which Finley had increased with wise investments, making a comfortable living for himself. He joined the army soon after he left university.

His athletic and powerful body made him an expert soldier in the special forces. Finley was unobtrusive, despite his great height. His tall frame and strong, manly features gave him a handsome but rugged look. But the man was clever, too. He had risen to the rank of captain while serving in Afghanistan during hair-raising assignments. Four years ago, he was wounded on a mission, and he decided that a desk job in the army was not for him. He'd returned home to Oxford to join Zac's business instead; his clever mind made him a brilliant strategist and intelligence specialist, his abilities useful to Zac's company. So when Finley left the army, it was a natural conclusion to join Zac's security firm.

Zac always asked when his friend slept, as Finley was up at all times, day or night. More recently, they became partners in the security firm, in readiness for Finley to take over the company when Zac succeeded his father as CEO to his family organization.

Finley was a cool and rational man, a calm fellow, and since he had been shot at by the Taliban in Afghanistan and had walked through mine fields during hell-raising missions in his army career, everything else to him, by comparison, was a walk in the park. Though, as much as he was all those things, the ex-soldier could be too serious and forbidding, almost harsh in front of a woman he liked.

He'd never had Zac's panache with women, but Finley wanted Kathryn. He had met her at Zac's wedding; she was one of Mollie's bridesmaids, and he liked her instantly. The spirited brunette had taken his attention. When they were in

Antibes, Finley had grown to like her even more, and by the end of their stay in France, he loved her.

Kathryn enamored him with her candor, her mellow nature, her simplicity and her purity of spirit. He had gotten to know her well—her charming, sunny personality, her beautiful soul. She had a positive attitude to life, practical, like him, and a childish humor. An enchanting brunette with long hair and chestnut eyes, and he worshipped the cheeky girl.

But the girl had suffered against Peter's violence in Antibes, and Finley had felt protective towards her ever since. He had even kissed her hands once, relieved she'd survived the upheaval. But with him being so much older, he wanted to be confident the girl loved him too, that it was not just a girlish infatuation which would fizzle out in a few months, that she wouldn't change her mind. And in his thoughts, young ladies were notoriously fleeting. So, he didn't want to expose his heart. But he worshipped her and required to be convinced of her affections. She was so young, and he didn't want to push her.

She was lovely to him, and she could do no wrong. Though, that night, at that precise moment, Finley was not too happy with her. Not. At. All. It dumbfounded him.

"What the fuck is going on, Zac?" he growled, "What the hell, a date with a man? Why? With whom?"

"Damned if I know! This is news to me, too. I thought you two were getting along fine."

Finley got up from his seat and rattled the chair. He paced the room, raking a hand through his short, dark hair. Even though he had a tall, massive frame, he marched up and down the room with agility and elegance in his step, as if he were a panther, ready to pounce on his victim.

"Sit down, Fin. Your food is getting cold," Zac said patiently to the man who was like a brother to him.

"Who's this damn guy, anyway; do you know him?"

"A student, I've seen him a few times in the house with Mollie, one of her classmates. He is tall, and I am about six foot two, but he is way taller than I am. He must be easily about six-five, at least. His height even beats you, though he is rather thin. You can take him, no problem," Zac scoffed in mirth.

Finley raised an eyebrow, giving him a fierce scowl. It didn't amuse him. His companion steadied his features again.

"Why is she suddenly dating? What's gotten into her?" Finley asked, exasperated.

"When was the last time you took Kathryn out on a date?"

"Well, I-I... What for, I say! I see her almost every night here, anyway, don't we talk, laugh and spend hours together, ha? Besides, she is herself here, relaxed. She gets all nervous when I take her out on a date. She fidgets and get so anxious."

"That's not the point. You have to take her out, man."

"Oh, hell! Yes, yes, I know. But I don't wish to scare the girl off."

"Scare her off? You are bloody ignoring her. Not the same!"

"Don't be ridiculous. We feel comfortable here. Besides, I think the chit is a virgin. I told you, I don't want to alarm her."

"A virgin?" Zac snorted, but another stern look from his friend steadied his features. He had known Finley long enough to realize it didn't amuse him to joke about his girls. "Well, did you tell her you like her?"

"I... well, not in so many words, but what the hell? Isn't it obvious?"

"It may be obvious to you, you pillock! But a girl likes to hear it."

"Bloody women!" Finley paused, but seeing the dubious expression on Zac's face, he went on, "Yes, yes, I know. Fine! But what's happening, a fucking date? The bloody chit! Where is she going?"

"I don't know. But I bet Mollie does."

"Find out where she's gone. I'll go and pick up her."

"What? Fin, that's crazy? She is on a date! Not a good idea. Wait until tomorrow. Speak to her then. Clear the air when both of you have had time to think."

"The hell, I am! Tomorrow maybe too late! Tell me where she is. Ask your wife! I am going after her."

"No, Fin, listen to me. You'll make things worse. It doesn't work that way—"

"Find out where she's gone; that's all I ask! And mind your own fucking business."

"Fine, your neck, man! Don't tell me I didn't warn you."

Chapter 3

"Hell, I've lost my appetite. I'm going home," Finley said, and a growl left his mouth. "Let me know what you find out from your wife, I want to know where Kat is," he added, irritated, to Zac, just before Mollie returned to the dining room.

Both men looked up at her, and she smiled. She was the image of innocence. Though she had a slight hesitation, she seemed angelic.

Her husband frowned at her.

"Good night, Mollie," Finley said.

"Are you leaving? But we haven't finished dinner yet," she said, and for a moment, she felt sorry for the man, that she had orchestrated this date for Kathryn, seeing how upset he was. But her remorse didn't last long.

"That's fine. I am done, and I am tired!" he replied, then he pivoted on his heels and left.

He didn't even ask me anything. Maybe Kathryn is right. The man is cold! she thought.

Mollie sat at the table and resumed her dinner, directing a sweet smile at her husband.

But Zac had a dubious expression on his face. "What's going on?" he asked.

"What?"

"You heard me; what's going on?" Zac reiterated skeptically.

"I don't understand what you mean?" Mollie replied, her baby blue eyes looking at him as if she were Bambi, wide and round as the moon. She had a look of virtuosity, as if she were a celestial angel who could do no wrong.

"You know perfectly well what I mean. With Kat," he claimed now, irritated at her unforthcoming answer.

"Kat?" she asked, professing surprise, full of righteous grace.

"Yes, with Kat?" he asked for the third time and began tapping a finger on the tabletop.

"Why do you ask?" she said, pretending total candor and sipping a little wine, but she squinted at him through the glass. She knew his tolerance might wear thin on this issue.

"Why do I ask? A date?" he shrieked. "Didn't you see Finley left? Upset, I might add." His patience was on the line as he frowned at her, and she couldn't help a guilty blush as red as her hair.

"Well, why are you and Fin so bewildered at the fact that my friend has a date? Why?"

"Yes, I am shocked. Haven't you seen them all these months? The two of them seemed like lovebirds. Now, all of a sudden, she has a date?"

"Don't you think she is beautiful enough to have a date, then? To have admirers, ha?"

"Mollie, that's not what I meant, and you know it. She is charming; she is stunning! Of course, she can, but why would she, when she likes Fin? And he feels the same about her. So, I am asking you, what's going on?"

"Nothing is going on. You said it yourself. She is gorgeous.

She is a free agent, no boyfriend. A man has asked her out, and she said yes. Nothing too complicated about that."

"A free agent? No boyfriend? What the devil are you talking about? What the hell is going on? I am not asking you again."

"Oh, bloody hell, not that again. I just told you."

"For your information, Finley likes her. A lot, I might add, and you know it! I thought she liked him too. Why is she having a date?"

"When was the last time your friend took her out on a date, a proper one? Like a man should take a woman on a date, ha?"

"Did you push her to go on a date with that guy?"

"Me?" she gasped, sounding so affronted by the accusation, looking so chaste, as if she were the Virgin Mary, "No! Of course, not. Fin had three dates with her in eight months. That's all! You do realize that, don't you? Three, only three! And a girl can't wait forever. He hasn't even kissed her. What do you say to that? She doesn't know where she stands with him. I understand he doesn't have a lot of flair with women, but even he knows he must do more than that to win a woman."

"For goodness's sake, they meet here every night," Zac bellowed.

"Yes, but it's not a date, is it? Not really, not a proper date like girls should have."

"Did you do this?"

"Me, no! But she can't just sit around waiting for him when he feels like it, can she? He has said nothing to her, nothing! Not even now, when he could have."

"What are you up to, hey?"

"Me? Why, you! Oh, no. Don't pin this on me! Your friend is lazy! A cheapskate!"

"Lazy? A cheapskate?" Zac cried out. "Did you put her up to this?"

"Don't say that again, I am warning you, or I shall get upset with you now."

"What are you up to, Mollie? Are you concocting a plan or something? Where is she?"

"What?"

"Where is Kat? Where has she gone on this date of hers? You know this, and now you'll tell me."

"Why?"

"So Fin can go and get her," he said, tugging at his collar.

"Don't be ridiculous! What is he? A caveman?"

"You did this? Admit it!" He glared at her, his jaw clenched.

"At least the two of you, if only for one night, have forgotten about work," she whined.

"Mollie!" Zac elongated her name in exasperation. "Did you put her up to this date? Tell me where she is."

"No."

"I warn you. Where is this damn date? Say it."

"No, I won't."

"You'll confess this instant!" And his lips pressed so tight, they whitened.

"Confess? Don't be daft, man. I said, no. If he wants to speak to her, Fin must wait his turn now." And she raised her chin in rebellion, with a satisfied smile.

Zac narrowed his eyes on her, and his head dipped forward.

She knew by now, this little movement of his head, though she found it so cute and irresistible, was a warning to her. It spelt danger, and it never brought her anything good.

"Tell me. Before I lose my patience with you."

"No! End of discussion."

"End of dis—"

He stood from the table, and the chair rattled behind him. She raised her head to him, with her baby blues eyes wide, and she swallowed hard, then she rose too.

28

He went around to her side, but she ran away from him.

"I told you to stop your little schemes! This is not a game; it upsets Fin. And oh, you are in trouble if you don't tell me right now where she is."

"No." Mollie tried to run from the room, but he caught up with her. His enormous hand gripped her upper arm tightly.

At that moment, Mrs. Johnson came back into the dining room to clear for dessert.

Mollie tried to pull away from Zac, thinking the woman's presence would hamper her husband's efforts to avoid a scene. But he tugged at her and didn't release her.

"Mrs. Johnson, please leave this; we are done for tonight. And close the door behind you. Make sure we are not disturbed!" Zac ordered.

The woman gave him a quick nod of the head and an apologetic smile to the girl.

Mollie tried to look dignified in front of the housekeeper, but given the fact Zac was holding her by her upper arm tightly as if she were a naughty child, she tried her utmost to maintain her demureness and nodded to the woman as elegantly as she possibly could master in the circumstances.

Humiliation!

The moment Mrs. Johnson closed the door behind herself, Zac turned to his wife. "Tell me!"

"No!" she repeated stubbornly, annoyed at him for embarrassing her and trying to liberate herself from his grip, but it was no use. He had a strong hold on her.

"Mollie, tell me right now!"

"No. Sod off!" She tried to fight him by slapping his hand, the one gripping her hard.

"Fine, you've got only yourself to blame."

He grabbed a chair, sat, and flung her over his knees.

"What the hell are you doing?" she cried out.

"You meddler, can't you leave things alone? Where is she?"

29

he asked again, as he lifted her skirt to her waist. But she fought him, and they wrestled for a minute.

"You are a caveman, and your friend too! The two of you are Neanderthals. You should be in a museum as extinct specimens, like dinosaurs!" she yelled at him. "The obnoxious men's species, that's what they should call you. No, I am not telling you. Put me down this instant, do you hear me?" she bellowed amongst several curses that would have sent the most infamous of urchins in the world silent and into a paralysis of shame. She fought him bravely.

Zac raised an eyebrow at her expletives, and a hint of an amused smile ran over his lips.

"Tell me, or you won't be able to sit for a week." And he smacked her backside with a solid slap of his hand.

She yelped and screamed at him, "Ahh, let me go! No, I won't! Put me down!" More crude curses came out of her mouth, directed at him, to all his ancestors, and to all his descendants.

"May I remind you that my offspring may be your babies too? If you are lucky, I might add, because, at this very minute, I doubt your capacity to grow into the mother of my children with this foul vernacular of yours," he rebuked, with more thunderous smacks hitting her bottom.

"Shit-head!" she yelled, and he raised his eyebrows, but, again, he couldn't hide a small smirk.

This type 'of arrangement' at their stubborn little fights, had turned familiar to them, though they were sparse, but when these occurred, deep down they both relished the sparring and the spanking. They found it the most sexy of foreplays! Though they would never admit to it, they enjoyed it.

"Fine. Let's see if this will loosen your tongue." He grabbed her flapping arms by her wrists, with one hand, and placed them behind her back, while with the other, he pulled her panties down to her knees. He pinched her red buttocks roughly, and she shrieked, threatening to cut his manly parts, but then with his open palm raised high above his head, he landed a hard smack down on each buttock. *Swoosh! Boom!* The sound reverberated in the room—flesh meeting flesh.

Her breath hitched at the pain. "Ouch! Ouch! Stop. Put me down."

"Where has Kat gone?"

"None of your business, you moron!"

He spanked her again, twice on each round, pert half-globe that were her delicious buttocks, harder. Her bottom stung, with red hand imprints. The creamy, rosy complexion of her firm backside had big red fingers shaped on it, and he liked it that way. And he did it again!

Her ass was on fire by now. "You are insane; let me go, I won't tell you. No." The stinging on her derriere was intolerable, bringing tears into her eyes. But she wouldn't let her friend down, even in her misery.

"Fine. I can do this all night, Mollie, your choice." He smacked her so hard that tears now ran freely.

She didn't have a chance. He was determined to pull the information out of her. In Zac's mind, his wife would soon find out she had no right interfering in this situation. So more whacks crashed on her round, gorgeous, pert ass.

She struggled to free her hands, but he had them firmly clasped in his. Mollie could not move.

She protested wildly, calling him all names under the sun, very few apt to a lady's ears, let alone that came from a lady's mouth, while he smacked her cute little ass harder, again and again.

Her backside was beyond fiery red. She was in hell. It stung and hurt, with tears in her eyes. Outrage and frustration mingled, the more he slapped her butt. The pain built up until she could not bear the stinging anymore, "The Heaven's Arms, she's meeting Ethan there," she blurted out in agony, and he stopped.

She released a heavy sigh, taking a breather.

"Good. Easy, you see. All you had to do was tell me this ten minutes ago—"

"You boorish savage," she whimpered at him in frustration.

He held her on his knees but suspended the spanking. His open palm was on her behind, still, and solidly on it, warming her butt. Until he pulled his phone out of his pocket and placed it on her back momentarily while he texted with one hand, the name of the pub to Finley. Then he put it aside again.

She tried to get up, but he held her there tightly.

Then he rubbed her backside with his hands. He massaged her, kneading her buttocks. "God, Mollie, you are stubborn. You know you had no choice! You should have spared this to yourself. But I guess you like it, don't you? Hey?" he said with a grin.

The hurt was horrid, though the rub of her buttocks with his big hand was spinning her into a delicious thrill. Her derriere was the color of fiery flames. It stung, but the patting and rubbing were pure pleasure. Butterflies fluttered in her tummy.

"Umm… don't you?" he asked, and he whacked her backside with all his might right in the middle between the two cheeks. "Answer me."

A shot of desire went straight to her core, and she gave out a loud moan. "Yes, yes, but please stop now," she replied through ragged breaths.

He rubbed her buttocks, each one in turn, enjoying touching his wife's delicious bottom.

At least the whole incident had made her man stop working for a while, and he was now giving her his full attention. And she relished it, even if her backside was on fire and consumed by pain like a damned soul in the depths of Hell.

After the spanking, the kneading felt like heaven, though. Her insides warmed at his hands and mingled with the pain, and the more he rubbed her buttocks, a warmth spread between her legs. She became wet. For a second, her legs parted, and she heaved a deep sigh and a moan. A smile curled upon his face.

"Are you inviting me, darling?" he declared in amusement, but his croaky voice betrayed the substantial hard-on.

She turned to him with a pout, but she denied nothing. She had not made love to her husband for three days and she wanted him. There and then, if truth were to be said.

He sat her on his knee, wiped a tear from her face, and said, "Stop meddling between my friends and their girlfriends."

"I am not meddling, and Kat is not Fin's girlfriend. At least, not yet," she pouted, tears still stinging the corners of her eyes.

Zac raised an eyebrow and shook his head in admonition. He peeked at her butt and saw it was scarlet, his big palm, red imprints on her luminous peachy skin a contrast. He cradled her against his chest, pulling her hair back from her face with his hand and giving her little kisses on her nose and forehead.

"Jesus, Mollie, you are as stubborn as a mule."

"You moron," she whispered, and he laughed as he continued to massage her bottom.

The more he rubbed, it did something to her insides, mellowing her core, driving her insane with lust. As he kneaded her butt, she became soaked, her walls began throbbing with desire at every touch, and his lips brushed over her face tenderly, making her wanton.

He lifted her face and kissed her mouth, a deep, ravenous kiss.

"Meddle again, and you won't sit down for a month. Let them be. They are adults," he breathed out between kisses.

"But he needed a push," she replied between ragged breaths with a sigh, and she brushed his jaw with her lips.

"Aha, I knew it!" he said, and for a moment, their eyes locked. But then he smiled and kissed her repeatedly.

"What's he going to do?" she asked between kisses.

He stopped, drew his head back and stared at her. "Fin? I don't know. But I texted him where she is." He caressed her hair and her face with his fingers. "Knowing him, he'll debate for a while, then he'll go to the pub. Not sure what he'll do, but if you think I am territorial with you, you don't understand about Fin. He already thinks of Kathryn as his."

"Oh, God, he'll cause a scene and—"

Zac didn't let her finish as his lips met hers. His tongue burst into her mouth, owning hers fiercely for some time.

She put her arms around his neck, clinging to him as they kissed until their lips were raw.

He stood, tall and mighty, and hauled her up with one arm like a rag doll. She yelped, not expecting it. Zac turned, and with his other arm, he made one big sweep over the table, to move things out of his way, and they clanked, rattled and clinked as he swept them away. Then he sat her on the table-top, while he stood at the edge of it.

He pulled her sweater over her head and ripped her cotton bra. *Trust her, she'll never get used to lace!* He chuckled.

"What? I didn't realize we would do this now, here. I had my lace panty and bra set for tonight," she said, as if she had read his mind, while she blushed the same fiery red as her hair and her butt, these perfectly matching in a scarlet tint.

He chuckled some more and pulled her panties, still dangling halfway, down and off her legs entirely, her skirt still raised to her midriff. He took off his shoes, shirt, trousers and boxers at the speed of light. She looked at him wantonly, sitting on the table, gorgeous as he was.

She dispensed of her skirt too. He kissed her ravenously, with his soul and body behind it. She put her arms around his neck and clung to him for dear life, both naked in the dining room, wanting each other, expressing their need, their passion and kissing each other fiercely.

He placed his manhood at her entrance and plunged into her. Zac loved his troublesome, sparkling, fiery young wife, and he wouldn't have her any other way, trouble and all.

"Oh, Mollie. I've missed you!" he sighed as he entered her.

She cried out his name, her breath quickening.

"Darling!" she blabbered amongst quick breaths as he plunged into her with deep, long thrusts. Soon the thrill became too intense for any rational thought.

He took one of her pink nipples into his mouth and sucked roughly, alternating with the other until they were both pert, dark and raw.

She moaned with pleasure, encouraging him to do more of the same. She mumbled his name several times, "Oh, Zac, Zac."

"Wait," he said. He wanted the desire to last. But she was ready.

He pressed her back on the table until she stretched out on it. He paused for a moment, staring at her sprawled on the tabletop with him inside her, panting, with her eyes full of love for him, wanting him, needing him, and his cock throbbed. She was his woman!

Passion struck them hard.

With his cock big and vigorous inside her, she clenched her walls around him, holding him and reveled in the feelings as he brought her to the verge of ecstasy.

"Wait," he said amongst short gasps.

No one had ever stirred in her the passion that Zac had,

since day one. She was struggling to contain herself; she needed release. He rubbed her nub with his finger, and she cried out his name again.

He kissed her mouth with pride, and when he ceased, he thrust harder inside her repeatedly as she gave small little moans, and her surrender made her tremble with pleasure. Her body quivered for long moments afterward.

He followed suit, his climax long and plentiful, murmuring endearments of love to her as the world whirled around them in ecstasy.

Chapter 4

"**E**xcuse me, miss, would you hand over the crisps, please?" the man sitting at the bar behind her said. He tapped her gently on the shoulder.

Kathryn was talking to Ethan cheerily, in full stream, when, at the sound of his voice, she froze. Her back to the fellow, she became speechless for a second, halting the flow of her conversation. She stood still, flushed red, but didn't move or say a thing.

The Heaven's Arms, I should have known! Finley thought. *Where else would a student take her. Damn Ethan, or whatever his name is!*

But she didn't turn to him. She disregarded his request, recovered soon enough and continued her discussion with her companion.

Bloody minx!

"Excuse me, miss, can you reach the bowl of crisps, please?" Finley repeated, unabashed, and this time, his tone of voice was raised and firm, reverberating over the hubbub of the pub.

"Kat, pass the crisps to that fellow behind you," Ethan

urged her in a huff, pointing his finger over her shoulder at the persistent chap on the other side of her.

She inhaled deeply and turned slowly. Her eyes turned narrow on him with annoyance.

Finley was sitting next to her at the bar, with an elbow on the counter, propping his head with his hand, while with his other, he threw a peanut up in the air, catching it with his mouth. He didn't appear to have a care in the world.

She gasped. Her nostrils flared. She scowled at him, with a long, serious stare that would have sent the devil looking for cover.

But his lips curled into a small grin, an amused expression appeared on his face. He was intent on mischief. Her scowl seemed not to have stirred him at all.

So, she picked up the bowl of crisps and crashed it on his side of the counter, hard, scattering half of its contents on it. Any harder, and she would have smashed the glass dish to pieces. Then she spun back to her companion and ignored him. But Ethan shifted aside for a second to say hello to somebody, and Finley took his chance.

"I'll give you two minutes to say goodbye to lover-boy. You are coming with me," he whispered in her ear while Ethan was turned away.

Kathryn blinked rapidly, assuming she was mistaken, but when Finley's words hit her, her eyes almost protruded out of her head in incredulity. It disconcerted her. She placed her palm on the side of her seat, gripping it so hard, her knuckles whitened and not knowing where to look.

The temerity of the man, she thought. *The overbearing lout! Insufferable, conceited, arrogant bear! How dare he!* She wanted to scream at him. And his sudden high-handed, dictatorial request was shocking. She didn't know what to do. But it infuriated her.

She spun around and glowered at him, "Get the hell out of here, Fin. I am on a date," Kathryn replied through clenched teeth and turned back to her friend, who had just seen her talking to the man.

"Is he bothering you?" Ethan asked her, glancing at the fellow behind her.

"Oh no, no. It's fine," she added with a thin smile and said something to move the conversation away from Finley.

As they conversed for a few minutes, she glanced furtively over her shoulder, but she could not see Finley behind her. So, she turned back to look and double-check, but he wasn't there anymore.

She gave a sigh of relief, but it annoyed her even more.

That's it! That's your attempt at getting me back? You hint at something and then you go? You leave me? You heartless, spineless lout. Bloody man lacks courage. He should have tried harder. Stupid man! After all that. No, sir, he's got no bottle.

Deep down, mingled emotions were building up in her. Annoyance, astonishment, she was furious at his cocky behavior. *This means he likes me, though, doesn't it? He must. Why else would he show up here then? Oh, Jesus, thank you!*

Her stomach did a somersault, butterflies squandering inside her, thinking he had come for her. She hyperventilated. *But he retreated soon enough.*

She scanned the lounge for a second, but she could no longer see him. *He must have left,* and she sighed, discontented, *I wish I hadn't told him to clear off!* Oh, God, she was so confused.

She was glad he had gone. She didn't want to cause a scene in the pub with Ethan there. She closed her eyes, not listening anymore to anything her companion was telling her.

But her annoyance rose again. *Good riddance. The boldness of the beast. How dare he? Now, he follows me because I am with another man? When he had eight months to make his move? Very well, I'll show him!* Her thoughts were twirling in her head.

One second, she was glad he had been there, and the next, she was mad at him for his audacity and appalling behavior.

In a flash, through the corner of her eye before she realized it, she saw someone drench Ethan in beer.

"Sorry, mate, it was an accident!" the fellow apologized profusely.

Ethan's eyes turned fiery, but he would not quarrel with a lady present. The young man cursed, stared at the man, but swung to her and said, "Sorry, Kat, I am popping to the loo to dry this off. I'll be back in a minute." He gave the man a ferocious look before moving on. "Stay away from her," Ethan whispered in warning in Finley's ear, but the student was not the fighting kind, and he was off in a scuff.

Of course, Finley totally ignored the lad's warning.

It angered her. Kathryn's doe-eyed chestnut moons were wide in confusion, her mouth agape. It appalled her, and her lips moved, trying to protest, but no sound came out. She could only scowl at him, disconcerted. *Oh my God! Did he just do that? He soaked Ethan in beer!*

She regained her composure, straightened herself up tall, her head high in contempt. She flicked her long dark hair back in a jerky movement. "Are you out of your mind? Why did you do that?" Kat exclaimed. It alarmed and shocked her that a laid-back lad, as she knew Finley to be, was acting like a madman. She stared him down, but he didn't even blink.

"What? It was a mishap," Finley insisted instead, with a righteous expression, as if he was an angel of goodness.

"A mishap? Mishap!" She stomped her foot heavily on the floor, "Fin, this is absurd. I am losing my patience with you; go home."

"So am I, darling, so am I. Have you said your goodbyes to lover-boy yet? Your two minutes are up," he urged bluntly.

She snorted at his audacity. "Clear off," she said calmly but defiantly.

Though, this time, he scowled at her, and his deadly stare caused her to gulp.

But she would not be intimidated. *The savage, high-and-mighty cocky bastard!* Oh no, she wasn't. He'd had eight months to show a signal of love to her, and if he wished to say something now, he would have to wait his turn. *When I am good and ready!* She would not humor him. Oh, no! Not after his appalling behavior tonight. So, she did the only thing she could in the circumstances and drenched him with her beer instead, from head to toe.

"There," she said with a triumphant, satisfied smile on her face, "now, leave!"

Finley closed his eyes for a second, his head went back, and he let the beer wash over him with a black curse.

"It serves you right, you silly man," she added, her head up a notch or two in her own elation, her jaw despondent. Her eyes, full of self-belief in her righteousness, seemed to say *I warned you so!*

"That's it!" Finley said, and as if a spring had suddenly motioned him into action, he circled her upper arm and marched her kicking and screaming out of the pub.

"Let me go. Do you hear me? You brute!" she yelled at him as he flounced her unceremoniously on the street toward his car.

He said nothing. He was a pace ahead of her, just dragging her along roughly.

"How dare you, damn you! You despotic monster, leave me alone this instant!" She squirmed, struggling to get out of his grip. But he held her tightly, pulling her with him. "I am on a date, do you understand?" she wailed, while passers-by looked on at them in consternation.

He stopped abruptly and turned to her. "You *were* on a date. Now, you are with me," he said peremptorily.

She opened her mouth to object, but she closed it again, shocked. What the hell was happening? The man was out of his mind. Where had the laid-back, sweet Finley gone? Who was this beast? But if she had to be honest—she would never admit to it—she liked this brute even more. This brute knew exactly what he wanted, and he wanted her. It raised her pulse. But it troubled her too. She didn't know what to do. She was out of her depth with him.

Deep down, *oh sweet Jesus, praise you,* it pleased her. The man had run through all this trouble, to get her back. And in the depth of her heart, a thought stunned her, *Oh, dear Lord, thank you for sending him, I'll say my prayers on Sunday.*

She couldn't believe her own reflections. Her emotions were in turmoil, her thoughts on his dreadful behavior sending her into overdrive. One minute, she was puzzled and annoyed at his despotic demeanor and, another, pleased he wanted her, elated.

Had she gone mad too? *Oh, my, my… but no, the man had no right. Really, he didn't!*

No good, after eight months of ignoring her, to treat her just like a friend, granted, a very special friend. Nonetheless, he hadn't made a pass at her. The oaf, the arrogant boor, who gave him the right now, the authority? *How dare he?* And her fury rose anew.

Her phone buzzed. "My phone is ringing, stop! I need to answer this," she cried out.

He halted, but he didn't let go of her. He held on to her upper arm as if high winds were trying to blow her away from him.

"If it's lover-boy, tell him your date is at an end, forever," he said curtly.

Her eyebrows would have shot out to the moon, if they could have, given her astonishment. She answered the phone and kept her eyes locked on him. His face had turned inscrutable, but the strong grip on her arm told her a story.

"Sorry, Ethan, something came up, my apologies. I am so sorry. I hope you are okay after that brute drenched you in beer. I'll explain tomorrow. I'll make it up to you. I swear," she said sweetly, feeling awful for her friend.

At her words, Finley scowled. His eyes narrowed on her as he stared her down, but he didn't say a word.

She swallowed hard, but she would not be intimidated. As soon as she put her phone away, he moved on and dragged her with him until they reached his car. He opened the door for her and motioned with his head to get in, without opening his mouth.

Her lips in a thin line, she flicked her dark, long hair back with a disdainful air and haughtily sat in the car, as if she were the Queen of England entering the royal carriage. She looked ahead with a haughty expression on her face.

When he didn't take the road to her house, but the Woodstock Road, she said, "Where the hell are we going?"

But he didn't answer.

"Where are we going, I said?" she urged again.

"My apartment."

"Your home? What for?"

"Because I don't trust lover-boy. You will be safe from him there."

"Safe? What makes you think I want to be safe from him?" she spat.

Finley snapped his head to her and gave her a fiery look. The burning in his green eyes scorched her.

She gulped and turned her head to stare ahead again. Though, suddenly, she became so incensed at his high-handed tactics, she started to give him a piece of her mind. She began with "You oaf, who gave you the right?" Then she moved on to, "Bloody brute." It was then the turn of, "You obnoxious man, who do you think you are?" And so she went on for two minutes, until he beeped the horn of his car continuously for five seconds, forcefully, launching a terrifying glare at her, and she almost wet her pants.

"Enough," he said. His voice was calm, though, and he was in control.

She had a feeling keeping her mouth shut at that moment would be her best option. That look scared the hell out of her, but oh my, she felt something steer down below, between her legs. Her pussy throbbed with a heavy warmth and she crossed her legs tightly. She would have sworn a little drip of wetness ran down her thighs.

But she stayed silent until they got to this house.

What they hadn't realized, as they were absorbed by the hubbub of their tempestuous evening, a woman in the pub had witnessed the entire scene between them. She had followed them into the street, got into her car, and she was now following them, discreetly, at a distance.

The woman had an inkling where they were going; she knew the way. She followed them until they reached Finley's apartment.

There, she stopped and waited in her car.

Fin waited for Kathryn to get out of the vehicle. They were in the underground carpark of his apartment block, on the outskirts, on the north side of Woodstock Road.

He got hold of her wrist and pulled her with him, but she shook him off.

"Don't touch me!" she growled.

He put his hands up with a small bow of the head, and with a tiny smile, he pointed the way to the elevator. In the lift, on their way up to his apartment, one moment, he was caressing the length of her body with his eyes, riveting on her, and the next, when she locked defiant eyes on him, he narrowed them into slits. He was losing patience with the minx. In particular, he had not liked her comment about not wishing to be safe from Ethan and wanting to make it up to him. Finley didn't like that one bit. The thought of Kathryn in the arms of another man was a definite no. Even less, had Finley liked all her wild name calling. She was out of order. Where had his sweet girl gone? His kitten had suddenly shown her claws, and she was feisty, naughty and mischievous.

He raked a hand through his short hair, though if he had to be honest, he admired this new side of her. He didn't necessarily like it, but it was exciting. Of course, he would never admit to it. He was enjoying sparring with her.

He opened his arms wide to the side, to touch the walls of the elevator with his palms, rising to his full height. Finley seemed massive, menacing, as if he were a hawk about to take off, and she was his prey to play with. He focused on her, and this time there was no hint of a smile or humor anywhere. His eyes were hard and unyielding, chastising her.

Kathryn lifted her head in defiance, her lips in a thin line of displeasure, and she stared back at him, but his eyes were too powerful, like a magnetic force, and he glared her down. She swallowed heavily and flushed. She bit her bottom lip and looked at her feet, toying with a tiny piece of fluff with her foot on the floor. She was nervous.

He opened the door of the lift with a key, and it landed them straight into his apartment. He gestured her in.

She dithered for a second. She had never been to his apartment before. In fact, even though they had spent most evenings together for eight months, in Mollie's house, she knew little about him other than the obvious—he was a reserved man—while he already knew all there was to know about her.

He motioned again impatiently.

She heaved and walked in. The reality was, for eight months, they had pussy-footed around each other and now they were about to come to roost.

"What do you suppose you'll do to me here? Don't even think of it, you rude, arrogant snake," she said when she turned to him.

"I told you, we need to talk, and that's what we'll do. But after I have a shower, given some silly girl threw a full pint of beer over me."

"I would have kicked your ass, too. But I didn't wish to cause a scene," she said, despondent, but it just seemed to amuse him.

"Oh, throwing beer over people is not causing a scene then?"

"Don't lecture me; you started this. You are using heavy-handed tactics, and let me tell you, this has not scored a single point in your favor."

"Points? I assumed we were past that."

"Past what? We are past nothing. We just have friends in common, that's all," she said, sounding all high and mighty.

He closed his eyes with a sigh. Then he gave her that look again, the glare of iron and ice that seemed to say, *you are playing with fire.* The one that could chill the polar caps twice over. It froze her. Those eyes rebuked her without a single word. It alarmed her, and it thrilled her, and in a flash, his green eyes turned on her, full of fire and heat. His desire felt, to her, palpable, and something between her legs warmed deliciously. What the hell was that?

With wandering eyes, she flushed, her gaze moving away from him. She didn't know where to turn, embarrassed at her sudden lust for this man. After his unseemly behavior, it wouldn't do.

"A drink while I have a shower?" he offered, "On second thought, I suspect you already have had too much to drink. Just sit down and relax; I won't be long," he said, his full laid-back persona in place again, the one she knew well. He sauntered toward his bedroom.

She relaxed and exhaled. By God, he irritated her, though. The brute had treated her like his possession. *How dare he?* He had ruined her date with Ethan. She was certain the young lad would not want to talk to her ever again, let alone date her. She would have to apologize profusely.

Then, the ape had hauled her out of the pub as if he was her master, bundling her into his car as if she were a package. *Jesus, the look he gave me in the lift, the glare of iron and ice.* It scared her and made her wet all at once. That look was new. It excited her and alarmed her. She had a little dribble come out of her pussy.

Good heavens, what was this man doing to her? She glanced around the room, not really seeing much, too nervous to note anything. She was trying to keep her mind off the warmth that had taken place at her core. Could this be happening to her? It soaked her. Her insides were doing somersaults because of him.

For a moment, something throbbed between her legs, butterflies fluttered in her tummy, and she longed to wrap herself around his frame. She craved... why, he could plunge into her, now, on this sofa. Not that she had experienced how that might feel. She had no clue; with all her bravado, she was still a virgin. She was a little ashamed of it, given she was nearly twenty-two years old, but she had wanted no man long enough to do it with. But at that precise minute, she would have caved in easily with Finley.

She was on tenterhooks with this man! *Sweet baby Jesus!* Could tonight go that way? For the love of God, deep down, she wasn't ready to do it for real. Oh, she had fantasized plenty about it, but now she might be on the verge of sex for real... she got nervous.

Here she was, in his apartment, and he wished to talk? *Oh God, if he only knew,* but the sweet man she had known for these past few months had transformed into the devil himself in the bar. Now the gentleman was back. She realized there were two sides to him, and if she had to admit, she embraced them both. The handsome gentleman she had learned to admire and bask in his company over the months had turned into an authoritarian despot, a caveman. What had suddenly caused this? *Me? No!*

They had had countless evenings at Mollie's. Every time, she'd had the best time. They played cards, chess, guffawing, enjoying the friendship. Kathryn idolized him, but this was invariably in the company of their friends, never alone. *That was his fault, though, not hers.*

But she craved him. She adored his smile, his booming laugh, the twinkle in his green, sexy eyes. The smile came with even, pearly teeth, framed by the most perfect lips... a tad too fleshy, but all the better. She was sure they could kiss divinely, be soft. She'd wished many times those lips could ravish hers.

She loved his eyes, vibrant green as leaves in the spring, full of life. When those eyes landed on her tonight, they had turned dark and mysterious, reminding her of the enchanting green woodlands of the Kielder Forest in Northumberland. She had once visited the forest with her parents when she was a child, and the deep green of the woodlands, the unsettling shadows cascading through them, the rays of light filtering through, the hazy mist in the afternoon, reminded her of his mysterious, dark green eyes at specific moments, as in the look he gave her when they were in the lift, and the one just before he went for his shower. When he looked at her that way, she would have done anything under those spellbinding eyes.

It mesmerized her. He hypnotized her. She would be his slave if he asked her. She worshipped him, she had to admit. But she was with a lad who could be possessed by craziness, as if an untamed spirit had a permanent residence in her gentle giant and only emerged at certain times and exploded without warning.

Oh dear God, what did I get myself into? For Heaven's sake, she was out of her depth with this man. And now, here she was, after all these months at his mercy, alone with him. *And he may turn wild again…* She gulped!

Suddenly, she stood up and glanced around. She became way too nervous and anxious. Perspiration mounted on her upper lip.

She looked at his elegant, modern apartment, so manly, and minimalist, like he had been tonight. Well, his behavior had not been elegant, but minimalist, yes. She plopped on the black sofa again. It was as soft as a baby's bottom, but she didn't know what to do and inhaled deeply with worry. In minutes, he would be back after his shower.

She chewed her nails in agitation. She hyperventilated again, her heartbeat rising, thumping in her chest. *What will he do to me? What if he turns amorous on me?* God only knew how long she had desired this moment, but now it was upon her, she was chickening out.

She stood again and turned toward the door that separated

the bedrooms from the living area, when she heard the shower going. Bloody fool!

She gulped and went to the door that connected to the elevator, but he had removed the key. The door was securely locked. *There must be another way out!* She spotted the exit to the stairwell in the dining room, but that door was bolted too. His behavior was so underhanded, it exasperated her. He had trapped her in… *the damn bear!* There must be emergency stairs, but she could not locate them.

The devil, the swine! Beast! Her rage was growing again, at his behavior. Or was it at the fear of what might happen next tonight? She yearned for it and dreaded it. She thought she had been ready for this, for sex, but right now, she wasn't.

She had to get out, but how? She felt like a woman ready for the gallows.

Now! Out! Go!

He came out of the shower in his sweatpants, bare chested and barefoot, drying his hair with a towel. Surprised she was not in the living area, he peeked in the dining room and she wasn't there, either. He checked the door to the elevator; it was still locked, as he had left it, and the key was in his possession. Next, he tested the exit to the stairway; it was firmly shut.

Where the devil is the saucy minx? He sprang into motion and ran. The fire staircase! He ran to the large door, now wide open in the kitchen. At the back of the apartment building, there was an emergency exit, in case of fire, stairs that led down to the road below, to the alleyway. She was, indeed, in an emergency. And she had scurried down those stairs at the speed of light.

He jumped on the sill and ran after her, but his bare feet slowed his run. "Kathryn, wait!" he yelled.

She looked up at him. She was already more than halfway down the stairs, and a burst of pace moved through her as she ran faster.

He saw her reach the street. But by the time he reached the bottom of the stairs, he was too late. She had hailed a passing taxi—*the lucky minx*—gotten into it and was gone.

She spun to him through the back window of the cab, smiled and waved her hand at him with great satisfaction, pleased with herself.

He muttered a few dark, sinful curses under his breath, an extraordinary outburst for someone so laid-back. But tonight, all his behavior had been strange. That girl had turned him into a savage. That's what love did to him, though.

He breathed himself back into control and decided it was best to let her be for tonight. But at least he had ended her date with Ethan, and he should be satisfied with that.

The naughty princess! Escape through the backstairs, the chit! He didn't think she had it in her, and he laughed, proud of his young woman, because, make no mistake, she *was* his!

Chapter 5

Earlier that night, in the same pub, a woman in a grey wool hat, a dull blue coat and an old scarf around her neck ordered a Corona beer at the bar. Once served, she picked up her drink and looked for a table. She sat, dejected.

Erin Blake was tired and upset, and she licked her wounds with her beer.

It'd been eight long months since he had died. And it was long overdue, she retrieved her brother's belongings from the university.

The reason it had taken so long, besides her despair at her brother's death, was her parents had passed away soon after he had. Her mother first, and later her father had died, too, within weeks of each other.

Thus, her sorrow had been too overwhelming to do anything, plunging her into an utter despair at the demise of her entire family in such a brief space of time. It left her all alone in the world, with a crushing grief.

She could well imagine Peter's death had led her parents to

an early grave too; they worshipped him so. She was sure they had died of grief.

So, after months of wrangling with misery, that afternoon, she had taken the plunge and gone to Oxford, to the Physics departments, to pick up his belongings.

All that survived of Professor Peter Blake, her twin brother, was in three cardboard boxes in the boot of her car now. Peter's wonderful life, the one he should have had, cut short, murdered by the slut, Mollie, when on that awful day in Antibes, she had ended his life.

'Self-defense' my foot. Poppycock! Erin swore silently at the verdict. Her clever, talented brother!

Tears stung in the corner of her eyes, but she had cried long and hard all these months, mourning his loss and that of her parents. But Peter had been her twin, and there was a bond between them she couldn't explain, a hole no one could fill, a grief she couldn't contain, and she missed him every day. She felt as if a limb had been cut off her, as if a part of her had died with him, too, that day.

So, that afternoon, she had mastered the courage to get his belongings back from his chambers at the university. It had taken her hours to do so, each item attached to a memory, and her despair had only increased with it. Three boxes, were all that was left of him!

Her thoughts spun in her head to the time, eight months ago, back to the small B&B in the fishing village of Port-Vendres in south-eastern France, where she had lingered, waiting for him to return from Antibes.

She had waited for three days, anxiously, miserably, but her brother did not return. His haphazard expedition to reclaim Mollie, his ex-girlfriend, who had fallen in love with Zac instead, had been his undoing.

Erin knew his plan would never work. She had tried to

dissuade him, but Peter was pigheaded, and he had died for his sins. And there were many, no doubt. But he didn't deserve to die in the most barbaric of manner, and that slut had gotten away with it. That murderous girl, Mollie, with her husband and all his friends.

She had another sip of the beer, lost in her thoughts, until she overheard something which made her head snap up. It drew her mind out of her reverie.

"Hey, Cindy, is Kathryn dating Ethan? Look at them. The lucky girl!"

A young woman at the next table said to her companion, "Where?"

The other girl pointed at the bar.

Erin glanced at the ladies, then in the bar's direction where they were pointing. She saw a pretty brunette sitting with a tall young man. It was the name that had taken Erin's attention.

Her brother had told her of a student called Kathryn who had blabbed to Zac that Peter was Mollie's secret ex-boyfriend.

Peter had manipulated Mollie into marrying Zac for his money, though he had not counted on them falling in love. But what they didn't know was her manipulative brother had a much darker plan in mind for Zac. Peter's plan had wanted Zac dead, wishing to take over his life, to seize his world and Mollie with it, too. But her brother's plan failed.

Peter's resentment had been immense and lay dormant for many years, pretending to be a close friend, until it had erupted into this crazy plan which, ultimately, caused his death.

So, the girl's revelations had set a chain of tragic events into motion that culminated in Peter's demise and the beginning of Erin's unending sorrow. She had tried to dissuade her brother from his horrid plan many times, but he would not listen to her.

Kathryn!

Erin had seen Mollie with her brother a couple of times, about a year and a half ago, but she had never met Kathryn. She didn't know her at all, and the name was not uncommon, so this girl could be anybody.

Erin studied the charming brunette at the bar. Could she be that girl? The one who, with her big mouth, had ultimately led to the death of her brother. The one who had blabbed it all.

She couldn't recall if Peter had given her any details, to make her standout. Erin racked her brain, but she thought of nothing. She stared at her. Perhaps she should ask the girls gossiping at the next table if this brunette was Mollie's friend. They might know, although not conclusive.

Kathryn! The girl that unraveled it all for Peter.

Erin had known her twin's character all her life. She was well aware of what he was capable of. She had to admit, he had not been a saint, far from it. How could a mind as brilliant as her brother's transform a longstanding friendship with Zac into such a treacherous plan, back-stubbing that friend in the most callous of manners? She didn't know.

Why had her brother harbored all that resentment? His friend's richness, was it all that mattered to her twin? *I guess I'll never know now.* Ultimately, that latent resentment had caused his death.

Suddenly, Erin blanched. Her hand trembled. She spilt her beer.

Christ! God almighty!

She saw him. She had not seen him for three years. Erin had even stayed clear of Zac's wedding, faking illness to avoid meeting him again. But there he was! That night, of all nights, there he was.

It had been a short but pleasurable fling for both of them, oh so satisfying. But then it had waned out. It was her fault; she had settled for her then-fiancé instead, although even the relationship with her fiancé had fizzled out later on.

But now, here he was, in the flesh, after all these years. Finley! She watched him; she studied him. *Sweet Jesus, the fellow is as handsome as ever!* His tall, masculine frame was unforgettable. His handsome, manly and ragged allure, unmistakable.

He had not spotted her, *thank God!* With all those clothes to cover her, she must have looked like a bag-lady. No wonder the man hadn't even glimpsed her way. Besides, he seemed to be totally absorbed by the girl.

But look at him, a powerful Adonis, his gorgeousness made ragged by a harsh military career. He was fresh out of the army when she'd had a fling with him. *His hellish nightmares, poor darling,* she remembered. He had seen terrible things during his army career, and she wondered if he still couldn't sleep because of his bad dreams.

Good God! He knows the girl. He would!

And when Erin watched the full scene between Finley and Kathryn unfold in the pub, she knew who the girl was.

It's her, that Kathryn!

What's going on between them?

She went after them when they left the pub. She got into her car and followed them to his apartment. She couldn't help it, as if she were a moth attracted to a flame. She almost lost them at one point, but she knew where she was going… she would wager for it. Erin remembered where he lived, in this upmarket part of town.

So the bloody girl, first, ruins my brother, plundering him to his death, and now she has taken him! Him!

Not that he was ever her man. Finley belonged to no one.

The girl will find out soon enough. No woman will put a complete claim on him.

She stopped for a few minutes in her car outside his apartment block and closed her eyes. She breathed in slowly, deeply. She didn't know what to do next.

This is stupid, for God's sake; stop this nonsense. Go home, she told herself, *what the hell are you doing here?*

She pressed her sweaty palms down her old, drab coat. She looked at herself in the rearview mirror, then at her drab clothes. God, if the man could see her now, he would not recognize her, she looked so awful, *well… he hasn't!*

And she laughed despite herself. She had always been an attractive woman, tall and slender, almost as tall as he was, with dark eyes and dark hair. Her hair a beautiful feature, she had turned heads, but since her family's death, she had taken no care of herself at all. *God, I look like a harpy.*

She would see to it tomorrow, starting with a visit to her hairdresser. To the beautician, she swore, and she would buy herself new clothes. *Oh, Good Lord!* She looked pitiful! *For goodness's sake,* she should get herself and Peter's boxes home and be done with it.

Erin sighed. She switched on the radio in the car and was ready to go. She gave one last look up at the building and scoffed at what she might have lost and the silly situation. She turned the music off again. She was restless. She got out of the car to breathe some night air. It would do her good, clear her mind. She should head home. *Late as it is!*

She was inhaling deep breaths, when from the corner of her eyes, she noticed some movement in the side alley. Erin swung around and looked up; she saw Kathryn on the fire escape staircase.

What the hell?

It was pitch dark! A dim lamplight in the alleyway cast a shadow on her. How the silly girl wasn't breaking her neck on that, she didn't know. She stared at her getting down at speed. Erin went back into her car and lowered herself in the seat, trying to hide, and watched.

When Kathryn was on her last steps, she noticed Finley jump on the stairwell too, after her. The young woman was running away from him.

What's going on? Well, they hadn't exactly been friendly in the pub, with the girl throwing a full glass of beer over him.

Erin laughed despite herself.

But when Kathryn hailed a passing taxi and left, she followed her too. Now, here she was. Erin sat in her car outside Kathryn's house. For what purpose, she didn't have a clue.

She must watch her, find out if she was the same Kathryn, the one who had unleashed her brother's demise. Quite sure, anyway, but she must not make a mistake. What the potential mistake was, or what she intended to do, she couldn't say. Fate had taken a wondrous turn over her destiny.

Chapter 6

Three days had passed since her disastrous date with Ethan. The young man was frosty with her; any cooler, and he would freeze himself to death. He had hardly talked to her and only when necessary. *This, thanks to Finley, the brute!* Oh, the arrogant bastard had ruined it for her with Ethan. *That's for sure!* It would take a lot of coaching to get the young man at least back to the study group. Kathryn needed him in it; he was pivotal. Not only that, but the man himself, Finley, had not tried to contact her or see her after that. Or worse, he hadn't attempted to apologize, after his unspeakable behavior that infamous night.

The wretch! Kathryn was seething. *Who the hell made him the kingpin? Well... if he thinks he is, he has another thing coming.*

She stayed away from Mollie's house on purpose to avoid seeing Finely. If she saw him, she would give him a piece of her mind. Besides, she wished *him* to unearth her, and not the other way around! Kathryn wasn't the emotional kind, but he had manhandled her with no rights. The ape! So she stayed away from anywhere in Oxford, where she could bump into him.

Finley had acted abominably, so underhandedly, it was beyond belief, as if she were his. Oh, no, she wasn't. He would have to beg her now… she would teach him a lesson, the arrogant sod!

Good God! They hadn't even kissed yet, and he reacted like this, from zero to a hundred in one step? In eight months, all she had from him were three dates. Three! One, two, three! Nothing more. Granted, very enjoyable dates, even though he'd behaved like the perfect gentleman. These were sinless dates, very proper, not even a kiss. Then, suddenly, the moment she dated someone else, tired of waiting for him to make a move, Finley sprung to life and became the possessive man. *Oh boy, that won't do!* So, she resolved she would not see him until he apologized.

She was on her way home from her class. Though, she must admit, all she heard in her lesson was blah blah blah. Nothing stuck in her brain. Her mind was spinning around the events with Finley, and she paid no attention to anything her tutor or her classmates said.

Get a grip, woman, force him out of your mind. Besides, it wasn't like he had declared his love for her, in fact, nothing at all. Not even now. Still nothing! She couldn't bear it. It was driving her crazy. Even after manhandling her, she had gotten zilch. Though, being fair, she had not given him the chance either, with her escape.

But a niggling thought kept lurking at the back of her mind. She tried to push it away, yet it kept resurfacing like a bad penny. She, plain Kathryn, was a total match to this demigod, Finley. Her app said so! It had proven it to her in black and white., indisputable… Mollie had confirmed the data input was correct.

She had double-checked it for herself, twice, to be sure. There were no errors. Butterflies kept on coming into her stomach at the thought. Either that, or the bloody premise data loads for the app were all wrong. Her heart sank. But she had verified that too, twice, and there were no inaccuracies. No mistakes, at least none she could spot.

Unless... she, Kathryn, was undoubtedly his match. Unless, he was surely her 'top pick'. *Her soulmate!* She massaged her temple. She was making her head hurt.

To make matters worse, suddenly, the vision of him with a stark naked, well-muscled, powerful chest chasing her through the fire stairwell that night came into her mind. He'd looked like a young, athletic, handsome and dangerous James Bond, suave and hot. More butterflies crashed at her core. She would have liked to lick that wall of muscles on his chest. Visions of her pink tongue sliding up and down on those muscles made her hot. *God, what am I doing?*

Just by thinking of him, she was sweltering under the collar, and the inside of her thighs grew warmer, in March, no less, as she walked in the street. Preposterous!

She must stop this train of thoughts! *What is he doing to me? Bloody hell,* the man was divine, though. She couldn't deny it, not even to herself. And that look he had given her when she said she didn't want to be saved from Ethan... hmm... had he acted upon it, she was sure Finley would have spanked her backside hard.

And there it was! Something felt wonderful at her core at this thought, and she didn't even know what it was, but the idea of him spanking her ass made her wanton, wet. Her panties soaked at this vision. *Oh, what the devil, he has turned me into some sulky, horny teenager. But spanking?* she mused, and again, another drip came out of her pussy. She flushed a billion shades of red at her fully-awake wet dream.

Heavens, what is happening to me? She was a level-headed girl, studious and hard-working, always doing the right thing. Her mom was so proud of her, saying to everybody how her daughter had never given her a single moment of worry in her life, being so respectful, industrious and obedient.

She wondered what her mother would make of her now, if she knew the lurid thoughts that crossed her mind about this man. *And spanking?* That was a new one on her; she must speak to Mollie!

God, but Finley looked divine without a shirt on. She tried to imagine him naked. She turned her thoughts to a painting class of a male nude she had attended, to which she spent most of the time trying to avoid those precise manly parts that were now on her mind, Finley's manhood… to imagine his private parts in all their glory. She chuckled to herself.

Stop that! You fool! she told herself. *Oh, sweet Jesus!* If he could have this power over her while she simply walked home… she was lost. Besides, he had experience with women, while she was… oh mother of God… still a virgin. It mortified her. What would he think?

She heaved a heavy sigh. Her whirlwind of images of him continued as she made her way home in the middle of the afternoon with the feeble March sun dropping over the horizon. Lost in her thoughts, suddenly, she bumped into someone. Her mind wandering, she had not seen the fellow coming; she was not watching where she was going. So she crashed, head on, into him.

"Oh, sorry," she blurted out, a little stunned, and raised her head to glance at the tall man. As she looked into his face, and was about to apologize again, she froze, staring at him.

She could not move as the man's dark, hard eyes pierced into hers. Even when he moved on quickly past her, she remained there, petrified. She hyperventilated. Her breath escaped her lungs, and a small, delayed scream left her mouth. Kathryn felt a surge of light-headedness. The street whirled around her for a moment. She held onto a railing on the side of the road to steady herself, while she breathed in and out to calm herself. *No, it can't be! No! Dear God! Impossible.*

But a few moments later, she recovered from the shock. She

turned back to look for the man, though he was gone. She darted her eyes around the street, scanning every tall person, but she could not see him anymore. *What was he wearing... black? Yes, black.*

Kathryn ran, trying to find the fellow, but he had vanished. Had she imagined him? She searched frantically in the side streets, too. She was beside herself, frightened, until, in her haste, she crashed into someone else again. This time, she gave a loud scream and trembled as the fellow put his arms around her. She resisted him, fighting him like a wild cat.

"Hey, hey, baby, it's okay. It's me," he said, concerned at her obvious distress. "I'm sorry. I didn't mean to scare you."

She fought as if he were attacking her, but he kept saying soothing words, trying to avoid her blows, "Hey, Kathryn, sweetie pie, it's me, Fin."

When he was finally got through to her, she looked up to him. "Fin!" she cried out and put her arms around him, giving an impressive sigh of relief and trembling uncontrollably.

"Hey, hey, what is it? I'm sorry. I didn't intend to—"

But she kept repeating, "Oh, Fin..." and hanging on to him tightly, still shivering.

"Are you okay? What is it?"

"Yes," she mumbled. She was so relieved it was him, she had forgotten his arrogant behavior, so great was her elation at seeing a friendly face after her ordeal.

"I am so glad to see you," Kathryn whispered, and tears came into her eyes.

"Hey, hey, what's that? What's going on?" he asked, drying one of her tears, but then it dawned on her, this was the ape who had treated her like he owned her.

So, she pushed him back. "But don't think for a moment you are off the hook for the other night," she chastised him, returning to herself. But she was so distraught at what she had seen moments earlier, she couldn't even fight Finley with all the things she had in mind to say to him.

He noticed her distress and noted she couldn't stop trembling. "You're shaking. What is it?"

"I-I don't know," she mumbled.

He looked at her for a second, studying her. "I was on my way home. Come, I'll make you a cup of tea, and we can talk," he said soothingly.

Despite herself, the shock she had suffered in running into the man with the piercing black eyes was too great to fight anything. She needed a friendly face, a sympathetic ear, even if it was the authoritarian man, the ex-soldier himself.

Finley opened the door of his car for her. She went in like a lamb and was silent as they drove to his apartment.

"Kat, what is it? You don't seem yourself. What's the matter? Why were you running in the street, what's happened? You're still shivering."

"I-I'm not sure," she said, wringing her hands in her lap in apprehension, confused.

Finley noticed her fretting with her hands, then it was the turn of her hair as she curled and uncurled a strand with her fingers. She took deep breaths and had a glazed expression on her face. It was not like her. "What were you doing just before I met you?"

"I-I was walking h-home…" she murmured.

"And?"

"I-I…"

"What, darling, what happened?"

"And I bumped into someone," she said.

"Who?"

"A man."

"Did he say things to you? Did he do something to you?" he asked her softly, but the fire in his eyes betrayed his thought... if a man had done something to her, he would kill the bugger!

She shook her head.

"Did you know him?" She nodded. Finley had been long enough in army intelligence to consider how to ask precise questions in times of stress, coaxing out what had upset her.

"Who was he? His name?" he asked as he reached for her hand in her lap and squeezed it.

She shivered, glancing at him for a moment.

He gave her a reassuring smile and then looked to the road. "Who, darling, who was he?"

"Oh, God, I think... I think I saw Peter! Professor Blake," she replied and burst into tears.

After they arrived at his place, she perched on his soft, black leather settee, still shaken. He made her a cup of tea, and she sipped at her drink with a glazed expression. She looked so vulnerable and upset that Finley's heart tightened and swelled with love for her. He wanted to protect her. God help whoever was upsetting her, and if he found the blackguard... Though, no doubt the man was dead! She was mistaken.

Kathryn placed the cup back on the table.

He moved it slightly and sat on the low table in front of her, their knees touching. He took both of her hands in his and looked into her eyes. "Darling, Peter is dead. He can't harm you anymore," he whispered, his tone gentle, watching her.

"I tell you, I know what I saw!" she snapped.

He moved next to her on the settee and caressed her hair back. "It was a hazy afternoon, and the sun was low toward your eyes—"

"I am telling you, I recognized him. It was Peter!" she reiterated, and a sob escaped her.

"Shush, you're safe now." He kept caressing her hair, and she leaned into him. "Perhaps you were worried about something. Are you? What were you thinking about when this man appeared?" Finley was trying to make sense of what she said.

She flushed scarlet, her flush so deep, she was sure he had an inkling her thoughts were on him when the incident happened.

"This fellow may have looked like him. But it wasn't him. When people have something on their mind, well... You could not have seen him, sweetie-pie; he's dead."

"I know he's dead. Of course, I do. But I tell you, I saw him," she cried desperately. She stood up, indignant and pleading at the same time. Then she sat again, dejected, and placed her head into her hands. He came closer to her on the settee and put his powerful arms around her. It made her feel safe.

Oh, God, how good he is. She poised her head on his chest. She could hear his heart beating fast, and she glanced at him, at his mouth, to be precise.

He smiled protectively at her.

She pulled away. *Perhaps, he is correct.* She didn't believe in ghosts. She was a woman of science, no ghosts in her world. How could she possibly have seen a dead man? Finley must be right. Her whirlwind of thoughts and the light must have played a trick on her mind. She half smiled at him, still not entirely convinced, but that was the only explanation she had. She sighed.

"Hey, are you hungry? I'll make us something to eat, and you'll feel better after dinner." He winked. "I am an excellent cook."

So, they enjoyed dinner together, and it was indeed wonderful.

He cooked spaghetti, with a fresh tomato and basil sauce. It was mouth-watering, light and fresh. The aroma of the basil permeated the dining room. She inhaled deeply with wide nostrils and woofed it down in a jiffy, the full plate of pasta. The stress had made her ravenous, his proximity even more.

"God, you really are good. This was delicious," Kathryn said with a satisfied pat on her stomach. She was finally at ease again.

She'd convinced herself it had been her turmoil of thoughts that had stressed her to the point of seeing a vision in the hazy afternoon sunlight. Could that be? She was not entirely sure, but it was the best explanation she could give herself in the circumstances.

There are no ghosts! And Peter is dead!

Though, it was Finley who had her at ease, made her feel safe again, made her forget what happened. He had made her laugh, relaxed her and made the evening fun for her, moving her thoughts from the incident.

Of course, it worried him, the fact she thought she saw a dead man, and Peter, no less. But she knew he wanted her to feel safe again.

"I told you, I am a great cook."

"But don't think you can get your way out of trouble just by cooking me dinner," she said, lifting an eyebrow when she had recovered enough for her gripe with his unspeakable behavior to return with a vengeance.

"Trouble? In trouble am I? What for?"

"You don't believe all is well, surely, after your behavior the other night? I tell you, it isn't. I am waiting for an apology after your dreadful actions."

"Apology? When I saved you from lover-boy?" he asked with a half smirk on his face.

She narrowed her eyes on him and didn't smile, fixing him with a harsh stare. He smiled tenderly at her.

"Oh, you are impossible, Fin! Apologize! Now!"

"You are the one who should say sorry to me, for behaving like a silly girl with this stupid date business and for throwing beer over me. Or have you forgotten that, hey? Putting yourself in danger by almost breaking your neck down the fire escape, I tell you, you don't understand how close you were to a good spanking if I had caught up with you."

She gasped, her mouth agape at the pig-headed man. Arrogant beast! However, she couldn't help but feel that warmth between her legs return. The vision of him thrashing her butt made butterflies crash at her core, hot under the collar in the middle of winter, right there in front of him. She flashed scarlet.

"Apologize! *Now!*" she blurted instead, to hide her wantonness. She rose from her seat and stood tall and haughty, her chin up a notch. She looked at him as if she was about to shoot arrows from her eyes.

"Sit; we have dessert to get through," he said, not even stirred.

"I want an apology now, or I am leaving," she repeated, stamping her foot.

"Sit!" he ordered, his voice loud, clear and peremptory.

"Fine." She stormed out of the room and toward the elevator door. In three long strides, he was with her. He pulled her back by her arm. She wriggled from him, but in her haste to get away from him, she backed herself against the wall, and he took his chance.

He pressed her to the wall. His body leaned heavily on hers while his open palms down to his elbows braced the wall on either side of her, thus trapping her in.

Her heart was thumping like a drum, rushing at a billion beats per second; she sensed it was ready to burst out of her ribcage. She swallowed.

Kathryn could breathe his scent, tangy, fresh and masculine. It was intoxicating, like drinking amber wine in a meadow on a fine summer afternoon, heady and exhilarating. She put her hands on his chest and hit a hard wall of muscles. She glanced up at him, and he gave her a devilish smile. The naughty twinkle in his green eyes told her she was the one in trouble.

His eyes darted from her mouth to her neck and back, as if he were a vampire in love and about to choose what to taste first from his divine muse.

It made her shiver. "Let me go," she murmured, not fighting him and without conviction. Weirdly, she realized she was in the right place, in the right arms, where she had hoped to be for so long.

But she gave a small cry when he suddenly tapped, gently, the middle of her legs with his cock. He teased her. He knew it would shock her. She gasped.

He smiled at what he had done. "Don't worry; I won't hurt you. You'll enjoy this, I promise you. But you must ask me."

"Go to Hell," she mumbled, still trying to be defiant. But she knew she had long lost her battle with this man and she would be his. Perhaps, even as far back as in that hospital bed in Antibes. She couldn't wait to be his, even if he was a brute at this minute.

An amusing smirk played on his face, as if he had read her thoughts, and he lowered his lips on her neck.

Another small gasp escaped her lungs as the thrill of his tongue and soft, warm, fleshy lips on her skin rocked her to the core. She quivered. The man was sexy, mean and tall, and she wanted him. He was her god. She would be his slave if he asked her. His lips trailed the length of her shoulders and returned to her neck. She stood still, delighting in them, her open hands on his chest sliding up and down in a caress as if they had a mind of their own, enjoying what they touched, despite her resistance.

He gave a deep growl, rather primitive, and she almost wet herself.

He pulled his head back to study her, his green eyes fired up and dark with lust—that look that turned her legs to jelly. It was scary and exciting.

"Do you wish me to kiss you?" He uttered the words softly, his voice silky, purring low, husky with desire, almost back to his gentlemanly ways, but with a sexiness that made her world twirl around her. His words felt like titillating caresses to her ears.

She nodded and gulped, despite herself.

"I want to hear you say it."

"Yes," she murmured.

"Yes, what?"

"Yes, please kiss—"

His mouth didn't even wait for her to finish her last word. It was on hers like a starving man who had been offered a slice of cake. He was ravishing her mouth and lips in an utter kiss that made her breathless.

Her insides were having a feast of their own at the pleasure, and the warmth between her legs expanded uncontrollably. Her breath quickened. She felt in awe of this man. Even his underhandedness was forgotten; it didn't bother her anymore if he could kiss her like that.

He pulled his head back to glance at her. Her eyes were closed. She moaned at the loss of his lips.

"Shall I go on kissing you? I won't be able to stop, you know, if I do…" he said.

She nodded, but he shook his head and caressed her lips with his thumb. "Say it! I want to hear the words," he murmured in her ear.

"Please, yes."

"No, no! I won't. Louder and clear, I said. What do you

want me to do to you, hey?" he whispered and tapped her lips with his fingers.

She brushed her mouth greedily against his fingers. She sighed. "Kiss me! Oh dear God! Kiss me, kiss me! Do what you will," she cried out, and at his slow, wicked grin, her breath hitched.

He took her mouth, time and time again, then feasted on her ear, neck and shoulders. His hands roamed the sides of her body, leaving a trail of fire on her skin, igniting the sparks that turned into a roaring blaze, spreading far and wide within her. From the tips of her hair, through her frame and limbs, down to her curling toes, her skin was alive with sensations so divine, she thought she would pass out. She didn't want his kisses to end, ever.

He opened two buttons and put his hand inside her blouse. Finley fondled her abundant, sexy bosom, and her arms went around his neck, drawing him to her. He squeezed her buds with his fingers. She cried out soft moans and bit her bottom lip.

His mouth found his way to her nipples, too. He playfully bit them, suckling them until they were pert and raw. Her plentiful breasts were a delight to him, and he reveled in them, sucking hungrily.

Her panties soaked, the inner passage between her legs was doing some delightful tightening exercises at every suck of her nipples, responding to the amorous pleasure he was lavishing on her.

"Fin," she begged. He raised his head to look at her. Her face said it all, but she was a virgin, and she wasn't even sure what she was pleading for by uttering his name.

He picked up the hem of her short skirt, and his hands were in her panties. She gave a loud cry when two fingers entered her.

"Fin," she called out again.

He pulled back, her expression uncertain. "I know, love," he said, despite the lust in his eyes.

What? He knows I am a virgin?

He thrust his fingers inside her, not too deep. He didn't want to take her womanhood right there; he craved to be in her when she crossed the pleasure bridge. But he wished her to experience passion at his touch. This, she was certainly doing.

So, he lowered himself onto his knees on the floor, raised her skirt, and took her panties down her legs, while she was looking down at him wide-eyed, mesmerized and panting.

She stepped out of them. "What are you doing?" she huffed and puffed in a murmur. She put her hands on his shoulders.

He gave her a wicked smile, a wink, and parted her legs wide while she stood there over him. His mouth went to her clit, while his fingers gently probed inside her.

She gasped at what he was doing to her and grabbed his shirt in her fists. Her chest heaving, her head back, her eyes closed, she was moaning like a thirsty woman who had suddenly found water.

He sucked and he licked until she was ready to burst, and when her blissful release overcame her, she called out his name in sweet little cries.

He continued to probe between her legs for a while, until she was thoroughly spent. Strength left her, her knees trembled. He stood up and lifted her into his arms. She was too dazed even to moan after her first-ever orgasm. A smile of content-ment came over him at seeing her like this, completely in his power, with the notion she had enjoyed every little lick, kiss and touch he'd performed on her body.

"Are you going to apologize now for throwing beer over me?" he whispered, nuzzling her neck.

She blinked twice at his words. "What?" she said, opening

her eyes to him. She didn't know if she had heard him correctly. "What did you say?"

"You owe me an apology," he repeated with a grin.

His words brought her back from heaven with a thud. "Put me down this instant!" she yelped, her smile leaving her face abruptly.

"I beg your pardon?"

"Yes, you! Silly man!" She fidgeted and kicked until he let her down on her feet.

"I was teasing you, love," he replied with a sigh.

"Teasing! How dare you?" She stood there, irritation on her face.

"God, Kat, it was a joke," he said, rolling his eyes, his hand akimbo. He cursed under his breath at his untimely words.

"You are the one who must apologize to me, for the other night, for behaving like a caveman. Now!" she said.

"Please. A poor joke at the wrong time; sorry. Can we continue—" he mumbled.

"Oh, you bloody think you are the king of the jungle, do you?"

"King of—" He scratched his head, and a curse left his mouth at this stubborn woman and at his imprudent, stupid joke.

She stormed off toward her purse, took her phone out and started dialing.

"What are you doing?" he asked her with a scowl and heaved, as if to say *God, give me strength.*

"Calling a taxi. I am going home."

"Kat. Please—"

"No. You are an arrogant man!" Even though his words had troubled her, the reality was she was nervous at the thought of making love to him, suddenly apprehensive again at having sex for the first time ever.

The indignation at his joke added to her old exasperation

at his behavior for the other night, but mainly, it was the fear at being on the verge of losing her virginity which had made her, all of a sudden, wish to find a quarrel with him. She was not ready. Anyway, he had been at fault first!

He stomped to her and pulled the phone out of her hand.

"Oh, you are something else, you are," she hissed at him.

"If you want to go home, I'll take you," he said coolly. He went to the elevator door and opened it. He motioned to her with a jerky movement of his head.

She froze, her eyes wide at him. She had a moment of doubt. *Sweet Jesus, shall I stay or go?* But she stood tall, raising her neck with a contemptuous stare at him. She scampered into the lift.

He followed her in, slamming the door behind him, which rattled with a loud bang, and he gave her such a disapproving look, she felt remorseful. Her eyes softened on him with a thin smile.

That was all the encouragement he needed. He closed the gap and took her mouth, bewitching her again by the time they got to the underground car park.

"Are you going to apologize to me, then?" she sighed into his ear, in the same melodious voice he had used with her earlier. He lifted his head to glance at her and his eyes narrowed on her.

When he said nothing, she tramped out of the lift. She threw a timid glance back at him, still in there, his head low on his chest, his hands akimbo. He seemed to debate with himself, but he followed her out soon enough. His key fob opened the doors of his car, and he jumped into the driver's seat, waiting for her to get in.

She glimpsed at him again when she got in. *Oh dear God, he is furious!*

They said nothing all the way to her house—not a word, though she was launching brief glances at him.

His face was impassive, like he had shut down. She couldn't read him. She didn't know what to do when they got there. He parked just outside her house. She was about to apologize to him, feeling awful, when he spoke.

"Sorry! I apologize for my behavior. For the other night, okay? I am sorry. Happy now? Hey? Technically, it was you who threw beer over me, but if you want me to say it, I've said it now. Sorry! Does it please you, then?" he voiced in a rush, his face in a scowl, like he didn't mean a single word at all. But he had apologized; he had said it!

She spun around to him, agape and eyes wide. *Well! He must like me then.* A small triumphant smile spread on her face.

"And I accept your apology. Thank you, Fin, goodnight!" she said, haughty and mighty, as if she were a seasoned princess, and she got out of the car.

Chapter 7

He didn't move for a few seconds; he sat in the car, still. He blinked a few times when the words registered as she left the car. "Goodnight?" Finley repeated, stunned. *The bloody stubborn minx.* "Come back here, right now," he yelled after her from the car window as she walked up the front steps to the house.

"I said, get back in here, do you hear me?"

Kathryn was glad she shut the door hastily behind herself as she entered her home.

He remained still, while the most outrageous, obscene curses spat out of his mouth. For a calm man, he had lost his cool thoroughly. He breathed in and out to control himself. It was rare that an experienced intelligence officer, an ex-soldier as he was, lost his calm so utterly. Over a girl! Though, it seemed, lately, this girl had the power to throw his calm out the window. *Damn.* What was his world coming to? She had even forced him to apologize, the strong-willed woman. She reminded him of a lovely kitten from his childhood, sweet and fluffy, adorable, but when it didn't fit, the kitten showed its sharp claws. This girl had pushed him to the limit with her naughty behavior. She even had him apologizing, when she was the one dating another man. She was the one throwing beer over him. The unacceptable behavior was all hers. All he had done was save her from going deeper into her own mistake. *The unreasonable, wretched creature!*

"Fine!" He got out of the car, marched up to the house, and beat on the door.

"Fin, hi!" George greeted him as he opened the door.

"Where is Kat?" Finley barked.

"Kat? She's out."

"She just came in. I brought her home. Where is she?"

"Oh, I see. Then, she must have gone straight to her bedroom. Upstairs."

"Which one."

"Purple door on the left," George, Kathryn's housemate, said.

Finley walked in, storming up the stairs until he got to the landing. He glanced about him.

Kathryn was glad she had left him. The man needed to calm down. *A wonderful night's sleep will do wonders to cool him down and make him reflect on his bad actions. Besides, how could he joke about something so serious as his appalling behavior? Well, he apologized.* The small triumphant smile was still on her face. *Great!* By God, he'd looked furious, though. *Anyhow, those lips have apologized,* she realized, pleased with herself.

Even if those same lips had done much more than just apologize tonight… her mind cast back to what those lips had been up to on her breasts and between her legs earlier on. Her core pulsated again, and she felt the need anew. *God! What has he done to me? Oh boy. He's turned me into this lustful creature.* And a jolt of pleasure flashed through her frame, recalling his lips on hers. She would have wanted more, but the man needed a lesson. Though, if she were to be honest, she had bolted. It had frightened her... Sex had! She got scared at the last hurdle. *You chickened out! Foolish girl!*

Her own behavior confused her. She had to admit this was uncharted territory for her. She wanted him, but she was a apprehensive about sex. Kathryn sighed. *I'll end up ruining even my friendship with him if I'm not careful. Let alone anything else...* She couldn't do that. *Oh, God, what am I going to do?*

She dropped her green coat on the chair, dejected. She sat on it, about to take her shoes off, when the door banged opened.

"Fin!" She stood up abruptly and swallowed. He stood under the door frame, tall, mighty, and oh, so handsome. The fire in his eyes told her he had not appreciated her swift exit.

He closed the door behind himself and locked it, pocketing the key.

"What the hell are you doing?" she cried, trying to look brave, but she gulped, her eyes wide at him.

"You wanted an apology out of me, and you got one."

"And I accepted your apology, thank you, so you can leave now."

"Listen, missy, let me tell you the rules."

"Rules? What rules?"

"Oh, yes, my rules, and if we are going to do this," he swung his hand between them, "then you'd better abide by them. Understood?"

"This? What are you talking about?" she said, but he ignored her question.

"Rule number one, you do not date other men, and that includes Ethan. If you really want to call lover-boy a man!" He scowled.

"Fin, please leave, it's late," she said with a worried expression.

"Two, you do not put yourself in danger, climbing down fire escape stairs." He paused, producing two digits this time. "Three, you bloody listen when I tell you something. Didn't you hear me calling you to get back in the car just now?"

"I did."

"And why didn't you, young lady? Hey, why not?"

"Well, I didn't want to. You deserved a lesson." She smiled, pleased with herself.

"Right! You are out of order."

Finley pushed her off gently from where she was standing near the chair, took her coat from the chair and dropped it on the floor, then he sat.

All of this happened so fast, when he grabbed her wrist, she gave a small scream.

He pulled her to him and hurled her, face down, across his knees.

"What the hell? Release me right now."

"Well, my sweet Kat, let me teach you a lesson, too. One you won't need a university class for." To that, he raised her skirt to her waist. He drew his breath in at the sight of her bare bottom. "What the devil! You've got no panties on."

"I know; they are still on the floor in your apartment, you silly man. Let me go this instant, I tell you!" She felt humiliated in that position, with no knickers on.

"God, you had no panties in my car all this time? You wicked girl." He raised his hand, and then *swoosh*, he smacked her bottom twice, each buttock hard. He left a trail of his digits on her pearly skin.

The sting hit her harshly. "You troglodyte!" she groaned and wriggled on his knees.

"Troglo—what?" he said. *Swoosh*, the sound of his hand landing hard on her butt filled the room. He whacked her solidly, but this time he couldn't hide an amused grin on his face.

The first hard bunch of spanks on her bare bottom were extremely painful, and she felt she was being punished. She wriggled her butt, groaned and complained loudly.

"You bad girl, will you stop this nonsense? Will you?"

The bite on her butt was undeniable, unbearable. But a few minutes into it, as he continued his unrelenting smacks on her peachy backside, the pain receded, and that warmth, which lately, seemed to live permanently between Kathryn's legs, resurfaced. High and mighty, the heat spread within her frame like a firestorm, though the sting on her butt brought tears to her eyes too, and she made her complaint known.

"Ouch, you ape. Put me down," she yelled at him, while tears flowed, but she couldn't hide the pleasure, the throbbing and the heaviness she now felt between her legs.

But he didn't let on. He swung his hand on her buttocks. Four quick smacks resonated, her flesh red like the midday sun at the height of summer. Her butt turned into two half-globes of fire. It stung and hurt, her creamy peach skin sizzling and burning as if it were in the fires of Hell.

"Ow, ow, stop! Please…"

"Will you do as you are told? Leave this nonsense about dating other men? So, we can have a loving relationship, instead of arguing all the time? Umm… what's gotten into you?"

"Relationship? Really?! I don't argue; you do," she complained.

"Me?" He whacked her, hard.

"Ow, ow, please. Stop, please!" she said, the pain excruciating, pleasurable and arousing at the same time. Her pussy throbbed, but she complained all the more to hide it.

Her raucous cries caught the attention of her housemates. They rattled at her door.

"Kat, are you okay?" George's voice came thundering through the door. "Kat?" He banged louder on it.

"Christ!" Finley cursed under his breath, stopping the spanking. "She is perfectly all right!" he said.

"Kat?" Her flat mate was adamant.

Finley looked at her, and she peeked up at him as tears were streaking her face.

"I'm fine, George," she said in a croaky voice. "It's okay. Please let us be."

She had visualized herself on Finley's knees during these last few days, since he had given her that look in the elevator, and how this would feel. Now she was experiencing it, she didn't intend him to stop, not too soon, anyway, despite the fact her butt burned.

"Are you sure?" the young lad repeated in surprise through the door.

"Yes, thank you, George. Please go away," she said, mastering all her self-control for her voice to sound calm and prim.

"Okay, if you say so, but I'm here if you need me," George bellowed from the outside, wondering what kind of sexy games they were playing at in that room. He must get some tips...

———

"Jesus!" Finley said, and curses broke out of his mouth, but a grin appeared on his face. It amused him she had sent her flat mate away despite her complaining about the spanking. *Naughty minx!*

Even with her fiery backside, Kathryn glanced up at him, and a blush spread upon her face too, despite her contrasting emotions and tears in her eyes. But she did not move.

He massaged her buttocks, slowly, with his big hands. He started to rub the pain away with his palms, massaging and kneading.

The throbbing between her legs resumed harder and

powerful. She had never experienced anything like this. The more he rubbed her butt, more flutters crashed around in her tummy. And she willed him to extend his marvelous massage as pleasure rose within her, mixed with pain. Chewing her lips, she hadn't realized until that moment, this had soaked her pussy. She had gone so still. A dribble came out of her pussy as he rubbed her buttocks. Her backside rose a notch, and her legs parted, seemingly with a will of their own. She felt embarrassed at her own wantonness, at her own sensations.

"Kat, are you all right?" Finley asked, his voice now rather croaky at the vision of her beautiful red butt as she was offering herself to him.

She swallowed, unable to speak without confessing how wet and wanton she had become. She nodded, but her legs parted a thud more, as if to say, 'you are welcome here, my love', and her bottom rose another notch or two.

He beamed with delight. "You are a naughty girl; you are a saucy, disobedient, naughty virgin. How lucky am I?" He brushed his fingers along her opening. "God, Kat, you are gleaming wet." He thrust his fingers inside her, until they met her barrier. He gave it a slight push. "Ow, ow" she said with a gasp at the mixed pain and pleasure at her virginity.

"Hmm, we must deal with this, but not here. I don't want your housemate in the way. I want you in my bed when you become mine," he said with a grin, and her face in a flush became redder than her buttocks. "Did you enjoy what I did to you with my mouth? In my house? Hey? And now, the spank-ing?" he asked in his rich bass tone of voice.

He withdrew his fingers from her pussy. She moaned, dissatisfied at the loss, but she nodded with a flush. He smacked her bottom hard, again, and she yelped, not expecting it.

"Say it." He spanked her again.

"Yes, I did," she whispered. He put his fingers inside her

again, probing, and she moaned with pleasure, but he withdrew them abruptly.

She gave a sigh of complaint. "No, please," she heard herself say. It surprised her, as if someone else had said the words. She felt humiliated at wanting to remain like this, but she couldn't help liking it.

He pulled her up and sat her on his knees, brushing her hair back from her face delicately with his hands, and he kissed her eyes, her nose, her jaw, her sensitive spot on her neck, and then he took her lips ravenously, hungrily.

All the while, she gave little moans of delight.

He pushed two fingers inside her pussy, thrusting in and out, while his mouth never left hers. "Open your blouse," he ordered, and she unbuttoned it for him. "Lift your breasts out of your bra."

She gulped, glancing into his eyes, and the fire in them made her core throb even more in anticipation. She obediently obliged, and he took one breast into his mouth, ravishing it.

While his fingers thrust inside her, he suckled her nipples, turning them pert and hard as if they were little purple stones. This made her soon abandon any rational thought until she was only aware of his mouth, his fingers, and her stinging red buttocks. Oh, what pleasures in her body, only pure bliss at the center of her universe, and it was not long before the room spun around her. Her soft cries did him proud, as her orgasm exploded long and protracted.

For a while, she wallowed in his embrace. Sweet kisses followed.

"Right; let's go to my apartment. We have no privacy here. We have some unfinished business." He murmured in her ear, "I don't want George interrupting us again, when I make you scream with pleasure."

"Now?"

"This minute!"

"But it's late," she replied.

He raised an eyebrow at her.

She giggled.

"Do you have something better to do?" he asked her amusingly.

She snorted. "No."

"Anything else take your fancy?"

"You, only you," she answered and kissed him sweetly.

Chapter 8

That same afternoon, the initial stage of her plan became a resounding success. She didn't know what her second part would be yet, but she was taking one step at the time. It took her a few days to design for the first stage.

But the damn girl had turned as pale as a sheet when she saw her, or rather when the girl thought she had seen him, that she had seen Peter! She had made Kathryn believe it was Peter. Her expression said it all. Erin was sure of it, and she was pleased. She had been lucky things had gone her way.

Since the night she discovered Kathryn in the pub, Erin had watched her over a few days, and soon learned her habits —where she attended her classes, her hangouts, who her friends were. She had even followed Mollie from Kathryn's house once, to Zac's townhouse.

Mollie had killed her brother in self-defense, the police had said at the time, but Erin was dubious about it. *Was it all true? But I guess I'll never know now.* Kathryn had revealed her twin for what he was, a cunning man, and in doing so, she had set in motion a chain of events which eventually caused Peter's demise. Those two girls had a lot to answer for.

And now, well… they went about their lives as normal, as if Peter had never existed. As if he had been nothing to them, had never been in the world, the villainous women. How could they live, when her brilliant brother, her twin, had died because of them?

But she wouldn't let them get away with it.

Erin had conveniently blacked out the fact her brother had been a deceitful, cunning man, who had manipulated Mollie into marrying Zac for money, with a plot to get rid of Zac altogether and win himself a good life through her, once he'd disposed of his rich friend. But the plan had backfired on Peter, with deadly consequences. These facts counted for nothing with Erin.

Her twin had been a thoroughly bad man, and she knew it, despite her love for him. But the sorrow in her soul at his loss, and at the loss of her parents, took over any coherent thought in her mind. The hurt was too great for her to think clearly, rationally, to be her usual, reasonable self. Only sadness and misery at their loss filled her days, her brain clouded by suffering. Death! And they had caused it. These were the only facts that mattered to her.

Erin couldn't remember a single day in the last eight months when, the moment she had opened her eyes in the morning, assuming she could eventually sleep, her soul hadn't ached at missing her family. She felt lonely and in despair. Torment was all she knew, every hour of every day, and it was driving her crazy. She had to do something.

And those two girls had been the cause of her malaise. Kathryn was at fault for having revealed the truth to Zac about her brother, which, in turn, had snowballed the events that lead to her brother's death. And Mollie, by committing the deed itself, by killing Peter… *Self-defense, my foot!* One was as bad as the other!

Coming back to Oxford to collect her twin's things had triggered powerful emotions in Erin, feelings of revenge she could not foil. She had never expected to feel this way. She had always been the sensible twin, the responsible one, and these new feelings were scary, frightening. But she could not thwart them. She didn't know how.

Seeing the girls going about their lives as if nothing had happened, had only exacerbated her despair and the pain in her soul. Her agony had become unbearable, her torture excruciating.

So it was easy for Erin. With her makeup bag and her experience as a makeup artist, it didn't take her long to transform herself into Peter, to change herself into her own brother.

Erin was Peter's twin sister. The looks were already there anyway, the contours of the face, the color and shape of the eyes, the nose, mouth, her height, though she was an inch shorter, but it wouldn't matter.

She just had to make a masculine version of herself to look like Peter. Not too difficult when you had the basic physiognomy elements already there and exceptional skills for transformation. She practiced for two days until she mastered the disguise to perfection.

She had to plan how and where the girl should see her, or rather *him*. Though, it had to be a brief moment, just a quick glimpse, or she would be lost. Erin was too feminine, even with the disguise, to look like a man. *Kathryn mustn't see me for too long, or my plan will fail.* It had to be a passing glance, and then she must flee. How would she escape?

One of Kathryn's lessons at the Physics departments took her, afterwards, to the Banbury Road on her way home. It was perfect, busy with several side streets where Erin could park her car and make her escape. And she did.

She didn't want any other students to recognize or believe Professor Peter Blake's ghost was back in Oxford, though. Erin only wanted Kathryn to think so. The fact it was early March and a cold afternoon had helped her. While she waited, her scarf and wool hat had hidden her identity, until she was ready to reveal it when the time came for her to bump into the young woman on the Banbury road.

Erin bumped into Kathryn as if it was nothing, and while the girl froze on the spot with paralyzing fear, she took her chance to disappear.

Erin carried on, ran to one of the side streets, got into her car and fled. She covered herself, putting her hat and scarf back on once she was out of sight. She couldn't help it, though, and she drove past the girl to see her face. Kathryn's expression said it all. She was terrified, and that pleased Erin.

Chapter 9

Finley drove back to his apartment at a great speed that night. It wasn't a vast distance to cover, but he couldn't wait to get there, to make love to her. He had waited over eight months, and that was long enough for him! He had contained and mastered his desire all this time; now it wanted to break free.

"If you go any faster, you'll kill us both or have the police on our tail. You'll end up spending the night in a bloody cell for speeding. Slow down!" Kathryn admonished him.

"Sorry!" he said, slowing down. "God, I want to kiss every bit of you, Kat. Trust me, by the time I am finished with you, you'll beg me to do it all over again," he concluded with a wink.

She blushed furiously.

He knew it would shock her, but he was teasing her. He wanted her to break out of her shell.

RAFFAELLA ROWELL

Kathryn flushed scarlet at his sensual references. She wasn't used to this kind of talk from a man. On one side, it scandalized her; on the other, it thrilled her, coming from the man. Her embarrassment made her burst out laughing, though, she bit her bottom lip in anxiousness and in anticipation.

She realized her hours as a virginal maiden could soon be at an end, taking into account his eagerness to have her, but she wouldn't have it any other way.

On the contrary, this time around, she was determined… she had regretted leaving earlier on, anyway. *Silly girl!* So, now, she resolved, she more than wanted to do it. She craved it.

Yes, please, was the thought at his words.

It scared her, but she would overcome her fears of sex. In fact, she was sure now, it would delight her. She could still feel her buttocks burning, as she could hardly sit in the aftermath of the spanking, but the desire had arisen in her, and the pleasure he had bestowed on her was unforgettable.

He glanced at her, her eyes downcast, her face flushed. It made him smile with tenderness. "Don't worry, love, I'll go easy on you," he said sweetly this time.

"Listen, I am not…" she mumbled.

"What?"

"Well, I am not a… I…" She mumbled, peeking at him under her lashes, her cheeks crimson. She fretted with her hands, pinching the skin between her thumb and forefinger.

"I told you, love, I know, and that's okay. I mean, assuming this is what you want, too," he hinted with a mellow tone as he reached out to her with a loving caress of her arm.

"Yes, I do, b-but…" She didn't know what to say. She lowered her eyes, played with her hair, then tried to smooth a wrinkle on her skirt. She was nervous.

"Upon my word, I can't get my head around this. A virgin at twenty-two? And this charming? This pretty? This lovely?

How did you manage that? You must have had hundreds of admirers," he voiced with a warming glance at her.

She flashed a fiery red at the compliments, embarrassed at her virginity. So, she just shrugged her shoulder with a bashful smile, while her heart raced in her chest. *He thinks I am pretty? Lovely?*

His hand searched for hers and brought it to his lips with a delicate kiss. A warmth radiated in her soul for this man. It spread through her frame all the way down to her dainty feet.

"Bloody hell, you are like honey, delightful, my love," he said with a glimpse at her, before turning back to the road. But if she had seen the intensity in the depth of his green eyes, there was no mistaking his passion, his feelings for her.

They got to the underground car park in his block.

She got out of the vehicle, waiting for him to lock it, but instead of locking the car and moving toward the elevator, he came to her side and pushed her back against it.

He kissed her ravenously. His tongue burst inside her mouth, searching every nook and cranny, sparring with hers. His kiss was hot, insatiable, and a thrill ran through her.

He leaned into her, his body pinning hers against the door, his hands caressing the length of her arms. He kissed her with passion, ferociously, with all his soul behind him.

Finley wanted more and more of her. His hunger multiplied, intensified. She could feel it in her mouth. It gave her power over him. It elated her.

His eagerness and his devotion delighted her. *And to think I've worried all these months that he didn't like me.* She rejoiced to see how much he wanted her, how he craved her, and it aroused her. Butterflies danced in her belly. And with this, her own desire grew to wondrous heights, until she was feverish for him, no longer fearing her first time to have sex, but willing it, with him. So she responded in kind, offering herself to him.

Suddenly, he opened the door of his car and nudged her down gently on the rear seat.

She gasped, not expecting it.

"Fin, what are you doing?" she asked through ragged breaths, her chestnut eyes sparkling wide in surprise.

"Shush," he replied. He pressed her down until she was lying along the back seat of his car. He kneeled just outside, on the floor. He grabbed her legs and pulled her to him until her backside was on the verge of the seat, almost out of the car.

"Fin, are you mad? Someone will see us!" Kathryn uttered in dismay.

"Shush… relax."

She was wearing no panties; it thrilled her somehow to go about with no underwear, and this time, she was so aware of it. It made her feel naughty, really sexy, for a change.

"Fin, the cameras…"

"Relax, they're not working. They are coming to fix them next week," he said, giving her a wolfish smile. He opened her legs wide, planted each leg on either side of his shoulders, so his face was right between them.

Her pussy was staring at him, juicy, bright and gleaming wet, calling him, practically in his face in all her glory. He growled, watching her magnificent sex. "Oh, love, you are beautiful! Everywhere," he groaned huskily, and he didn't lose any time.

His lips went for her clit, sucking it forcefully. With the same hunger his kisses had unleashed on her lips, his mouth now feasted on her pussy with all his might. His fingers entered her too, as she gave him sweet little cries of encouragement. But he had to refrain himself in order not to defile her there and then. He sucked and thrust inside her.

She gasped and panted, her breathing quickened. For a flash, she thought it was way too sinful. She feared that someone may see them, but soon oblivion dazed her. Kathryn delighted in the thrill of his mouth on her pussy, and ecstasy took over any logical thought.

She would not have cared if the Queen of England had come upon them then. She squirmed on the back seat, relishing every bit of magic his mouth and tongue lavished on her, inviting him with little cries of approval to no end. It felt to her as if a whirlwind had vented on her womanly parts, spinning her in a vortex of passion, in a frenzy of delight. She twirled and whirled in ecstasy. Her eyes closed in total abandon, only aware of her body's pleasure.

Her palms were flat against the seat. She was dazzled by lust, need, and the pleasure building inside her. When her blissful release came, she cried his name in little, panting bursts.

Ripples of rapture continued to shudder her body for long afterward. Perhaps it had been the naughtiness of doing it in a public place that had made her so overcome with ecstasy.

She concluded it was his mouth, and the proximity of this man that was turning her into a wanton lush. *But hey, who cared!*

For a few moments, she lay there, not moving, her body limp. She was still panting while he watched her with satisfaction, totally done in, spent. A sinful smile spread upon his face. He had an idea this girl would be a revelation to him, and she was. Her chest was heaving, her largish breasts titillating him in the aftermath of her orgasm. He couldn't wait to suck them to his heart content.

Her hand reached up to her face, and she covered her eyes. He rose and moved over her on all fours, on the back seat; he was atop, looking down on her. He kissed her forehead with a lingering kiss.

"You didn't think I was going to let you ride in my car, twice in a row, with no panties on and do nothing about it, did you?" his low, croaky, husky, baritone voiced with an amused smirk on his face.

She lowered her hand from her eyes, blushed and giggled at the same time.

"You are a bad man, Finley Harman, by far the most wicked I know," she said, and he narrowed his eyes on her. He retreated out of the car with his feet firmly on the floor again. He pulled one of her legs up and smacked her bare bottom hard, twice in quick succession, leaving an imprint of his hand.

"Ow, ow, why?"

"How many wicked men do you know?" he challenged with a grin.

She pulled an imperious face at him, with a pout.

"Come on, love, upstairs! I'll show you wicked," he said as he pulled her skirt down, covering her modesty, and dragged her out of the car.

She roared with laughter.

He gave her another resounding smack on her backside.

She ran to the elevator with a squeal.

But he had the key. When he caught up with her, he kissed her ravenously against the wall.

The doors opened, and one of his neighbors got out of the elevator. "Good evening," the old man said, catching them.

They both straightened up, having been discovered kissing like teenagers.

"Mr. Morton, good evening, sir. Where are you off to so late?" Finley replied with a nod to the man, but his voice was husky and breathy, revealing more than he should.

"Oh, my daughter has locked herself out of the house. I'm taking her spare set of keys to her. I keep them in my apartment, and it's lucky I do."

"I see."

"Yes, I know, nothing too exciting, Mr. Harman, judging by your standards tonight," Mr. Morton replied with a wink.

Finley gave a sonorous laugh. He liked the man; he was fun, even though he was close to eighty years old.

Kathryn blushed and nodded when the man directed a sweet smile and a bow of the head at her.

They said their goodbyes and went into the elevator.

Finley couldn't help kissing her in there, too, as they went up. By the time they were back inside his apartment, she was panting again. She didn't know what was happening to her; her pussy was gleaming.

She tasted herself on his lips, a first for her. *But then there is a first for everything,* she thought as she enjoyed it.

They could not stop kissing, and as he did so, now in his living room, he shed his clothes fast. She laughed at the speed in which he got undressed. His shirt was off, swiftly followed by his shoes, trousers, left only in his boxers.

She wanted to admire him, almost naked as he was. But he didn't give her the time. He kissed her. His forceful kisses made her take small steps back until she was against the wall.

Finley unbuttoned two buttons on her blouse and found his way to her breasts, put his mouth on her nipples, alternating one with the other. He suckled on them as if his life depended on it until they were pert and hard, like pebbles. Finley and Kathryn were both in a feverish frenzy of lust.

She panted in a daze. He picked her up into his arms, making a beeline for his bedroom; she opened her eyes and smiled languidly. Finley kissed her hard and fast, his mouth owning her until her lips were fire red and utterly kissed. Then, he slowed down for a few moments.

"You know it will hurt," he whispered with a warm smile.

"Fin, I may not have done it yet, but I know what happens," she replied, blushing.

"You do, do you? Tell me when I am finished with you," he said cockily.

She slapped his shoulders. "You are impossible!"

"Seriously, are you sure you want do this? With me? Here, now? Hey?" he responded with a serious stare into her eyes as he deposited her down onto her feet. His green eyes flickering with fire, he stood there waiting for a reply. When she didn't answer straightaway, he got nervous. *Is she going to say 'no'?*

Kathryn glanced around the bedroom for a second. Though catching him unawares, she pivoted on him, and pushed him down on the bed, hard, with all her might. Both of her palms open on his chest, forcing him strongly all the way down, she made him lie on the bed, and she mounted him with a smirk of victory.

She placed herself astride him and kissed him ravenously like he had done to her, making her mark on him. Then she pulled away with a vixen-like, sexy smile. She was straddling him, and he was relishing her taking control, taking command of him.

Kathryn unbuttoned the rest of her blouse, her eyes locked on him as she took it off slowly. Revealing a bit of her skin at the time, she titillated him mischievously. She then undid her bra, raising her eyebrows to him. Her splendid, rather large breasts were now exposed in all their glory.

He growled, a guttural, primitive sound, at their beauty, and as if he wasn't hard enough, blood flooded straight to his manhood. "God, love, you are gorgeous," he declared, his voice low and croaky.

Next, she unzipped her skirt and got it off. He helped her with that. Then she positioned herself back astride him again, stark naked in all her splendor.

Finley wondered who in Heaven he had pleased to deserve her.

"What does this say to you?" she asked in a sexy slur.

"I guess that's a *yes*!" he replied, lifting his eyebrows and taking all of her in, his eyes gazing at her body in anticipation.

She went back to his mouth with a replay of hungry kisses.

"Jesus, I can't believe how lovely you are," he mumbled, caressing her hair back when they ended the kisses.

Her hands trailed his skin, and he lay there, reveling at her touch. Though she was not an expert, she was certainly keen. He slowed her down and took over, watching as she let the pleasure wash over her. In a sudden movement, he turned her over on her back. Finley was over her, and they kissed some more.

———

He paused and rose, his body calling out to her. She watched him, giggling nervously as he shed his boxers. He was a vision to her, so tall, with a muscular, chiseled chest and wide, massive shoulders that tapered at the waist, all held together beautifully by powerful thighs, long-limbed, and a well-built, rounded set of sexy buttocks. He was perfect!

Kathryn's giggles stopped when she got to see his massive, hard erection. She wasn't sure all of him was going to fit inside her. *Was it? How?* Her virginal apprehension returned for a moment.

He smiled as if he guessed her thought. "Relax, I will go easy on you." He winked with a sinful grin.

She blushed and guffawed, covering her lips.

He came back over her on all fours. He took her mouth, ravaging her with his kisses, his need and his want, his adoration for her. The passion was too explosive to deny it any longer.

The moment consumed her too, as she was overwhelmed by her burning for him, craving him.

He fondled her pussy. It soaked her.

"Oh, love, I adore you," he cracked, with a bass croaky voice full of desire. She responded by pulling him closer to her, thus encouraging him with kisses all over his face and neck.

He lay between her legs and started pushing inside her.

She hissed, a sound somewhere between a moan and cry. Acutely aware of his cock entering her, she could feel his strong-muscled body on top of her, crashing against her soft skin. She wanted the full weight of him with no restrains.

Her heart thundered. She thought it was going to burst out of her chest, feeling him inching inside her. Her mouth was dry, but she had desired him for months. Now, with him, she felt complete. She sighed deeply, releasing her fears once and for all, and she surrendered herself to him without inhibitions.

His panting grew louder as he pushed against her virginity. He struggled to restrain himself, trying not to frighten her, not to hurt her. He didn't want to overwhelm her with his force and need. As he thrust inside her, he eventually overcame her maidenhood with slow, deep thrusts.

She gave out a small cry, tensing for a second as he pierced her virtue. Her nails dug into his shoulders, but after the first few moments of pain, these mingled with other sentiments far stronger and sublime.

He paused to look at her, making sure she was all right and give her time to adjust to him, now fully inside her. She returned a tender smile to him, dragging her lips across his cheeks.

Then his eyes locked with hers in a savage expression of want and desire. He kissed her, not moving. Only his mouth told her how strong his passion for her was. He tried to control the need for her, to ease her into it.

"Are you okay?" he asked in a low, ragged breath.

She nodded with a coy smile. Her lips met his, showing him she was ready for him, needing him as he wanted her.

As he moved again, in yearning, long strokes, desire filled their senses. She parted her legs wider, in total abandonment, as passion swept over her anew. He plunged into her more vigorously. Her walls clenched around him, and his cock throbbed.

As he thrust in and out of her, he was now her man, she knew, just as she indelibly became his. She belonged to him now. They yielded to each other, flooded by love, lust and need.

It wasn't long before their climaxes came, exploding in their bodies, making them both shudder with pleasure until they were utterly spent.

"Oh, my love, Kat," he said, caressing her face and kissing her brow.

"Fin..." she murmured and just smiled, unable to utter another word. They kissed tenderly for some time.

He moved off her and lay alongside her. He propped his head on his elbow, looking at her, searching her eyes and caressing her body with his other hand lovingly.

She wallowed in the warmth of his caress, marveling at the adoring look on his face. That was new to her, but she liked it. She was sure he could discern a similar emotion in her eyes. Thus, they indulged in their newfound intimacy, enjoying their bodies' pleasures several times that night, until exhaustion took them over, and they fell asleep.

"Come on, sleepyhead," he said, caressing her, pulling her hair out of her face.

Kathryn gave a growl. She was not a morning person. He snorted. She offered him a small smile. It wouldn't do to be a bear on their first morning together, so she returned a peck on his lips but soon turned the other way.

He grinned. To be fair, he had exhausted the gorgeous creature to his heart's content, taking her several times and making her his.

I hope she is mine for keeps, for eternity.

"Come on, love. As much as I would like to stay in bed with you all day, I have work to do and places to be. Raise your plump, sexy ass from that bed, now."

"No, can't I just stay here? I promise, I won't do anything."

"No, I made you breakfast. You have a class to go to and some studying to do, so move. Up, you go! I've let you sleep long enough."

"What times is it? It's still dark!" she mumbled, avoiding looking at him.

"Six."

"Six?" she complained in agony. "For God's sake, Fin, it's the middle of the night. I have no classes until eleven o'clock today, "she replied, turning again the other way.

"I want to have breakfast with you. Come on, sunshine. Then you can catch up on your studies until then. Rise and shine, my love."

"God, Mollie warned me. She said you don't bloody sleep! She thinks you are not human."

"Does she now? Well, I suppose given what we did last night and the amount of it, she might just have a point there," he said, deadpan.

She roared with laughter and turned to him. She put her arms around his neck, kissed him wantonly and seductively, repeatedly.

But if he thought he was going to have his usual routine with her between his arms, he was mistaken.

Thus, they remained in bed until ten o'clock. He postponed his work and embarked on his explosive lovemaking with eagerness instead.

Chapter 10

Two days later, Fin was in Zac's office in a meeting. There was a commotion outside, and the oak double doors flapped open with a bang. They ricocheted on the wall.

The men looked up at the newcomer in confusion. Few people dared to interrupt Zac in that manner.

A tall, elegant man in a blue, perfectly cut and stylish suit to enhance his graceful, masculine assets, invaded the room with resolute strides. He didn't look happy.

His hair seemed dark, flowing long as he walked with purpose, but at a closer inspection, the rich russet hues in it made it a remarkable, glorious tone, his chiseled good looks sculpted to perfection, with high cheekbones to die for. This fellow was imposing.

That day, his pale blue eyes had an unmistakable murderous glint in them, and it confirmed him as a man you would not overlook for his beauty and temper, accustomed, as he was, to boss people around to get his way.

Gladys, Zac's secretary, fluffed behind him, struggling to

catch up with him. "My Lord, you cannot come in here. Mr. Sorensen is busy, sir, please?"

"Buck! What the devil?" Zac said, looking at him, using the man's old Etonian nickname.

"Lord Buckley," Finley joined, surprised, adopting the fellow's proper title to appease him, because clearly, something was bothering the man, and he was indeed the son and heir of an earl.

"I am so sorry, Mr. Sorensen, but I couldn't stop—" his secretary tried apologetically.

"That's okay, Gladys. You can go. I'll deal with this."

"Sorensen! You need to get a grip on your wife and that friend of hers! What's her name… well… Anyway, are the silly girls trying to ruin me?" the young aristocrat said the moment the woman left the room.

"Do you mean Kathryn?" Finley whispered with foreboding.

"That's it, Kathryn, and Mollie. Jesus, what are those two up to? Who the hell gave them permission to interfere in my life? Sorensen, you need to control your wife. Can't you handle her?" he retorted with a vicious smirk.

"Gus, what's going on? Mollie? What do you want with her? With them?" Zac said, using the man's nickname, trying to placate the furious Lord.

"Me, with them? Oh no, no. It's them, with me. That's what I am asking you. What the hell do they want with me?"

"Are you sure you got this right? My wife? Mollie? I don't understand."

"Well, maybe you should pay more attention to your wife and the friends she keeps. Perhaps then you would realize what she's up to," Fergus said.

This irked the two men.

"What the hell's gotten into you?" Zac blustered. The

fellow could be so full of himself, he was annoying him now by barging into his office, sermonizing him about his wife.

To be fair, it didn't surprise Zac too much. *Is Mollie back to her old mischiefs? Hmm...* She had not put a foot wrong for months. *If I ignore her meddling between Kathryn and Finley.* But knowing his lively girl, he had an inkling this was not her only peccadillo. He wondered what that wild, mischievous, adorable wife of his had done this time.

"Gentlemen, gentlemen, please. Shall we sit and calm down? Let's see if we can understand each other. Shall we?" Finley urged, looking at them, trying to smooth over the two men at loggerheads. Though, if he had to admit it, he was irritated too. Kathryn seemed to be involved in this, whatever it was about. And if it infuriated the young aristocrat, well... it couldn't be good.

"Yes, that Kathryn girl, too. To think the troublemaker was an intern in my firm, the foolish girl! And your wife, Zac! The two of them, what the heck are they putting ideas into my father's head about matching me up with some floozy on their app? I am warning you. Tell them to stay out of my life! Do you hear me? My father is crazy; the old cantankerous fool is going balmy, but have they lost their minds, too?"

"What are you talking about?"

"Mollie and that friend of hers have convinced my father I need a wife. They told him they can pair me up with some girl. And my incredibly annoying father has listened to them. The old fog has gotten this into his head. He is asking that I marry whoever they'll match me up... God knows, what the hell he is thinking! Do you understand? Who the hell told them they could do this? I swear, I am suing you, see if I won't. Tell them to stop this foolishness now. Understood? Before it gets out of hand," Fergus said, flashing his pale blue eyes at them. There was no mistaking his warning.

Zac rubbed a hand over his face. He looked at Finley and then at Fergus, and his eyes widened.

"Oooh…" was the reply from Zac and Finley in unison.

The penny had finally dropped. It clicked what the man was annoyed about. They didn't like it one bit. Both men knew Kathryn and Mollie were working on the app project, though they had not paid too much attention to the details. They had dismissed it as the girls' pastime, something they did amongst their friends at university. But tackling Gus? None other than Fergus Waltham, the heir to the Earl of Buckley? The earl's son? And against his knowledge? God Almighty, there was no end to the girls' mischief. This man was another kettle of fish.

Gustave Waltham, Earl of Buckley, was ill. Everyone knew the old fellow might not be long to this world. He had been ill for some time. People thought he might not recover. So, in his illness, the old man wished to see his heir settled. He wanted to go to his grave knowing that the irascible, ill-tempered, crotchety son of his, *Fergus,* had a woman to look after him, and in turn, to produce the next heir, too.

He had pushed Fergus, or Gus, as he was known to his friends, to marry for a long time but to no avail. The young Lord was against marriage. At times, it even seemed to his father he was against women.

So Gustave had taken it upon himself to solve the issue and take his chances with Mollie and Kathryn's app without his son's knowledge.

However, for the girls to meddle in this was awful news for Zac and Finley's company. Buckley was one of their best clients, and to upset him would be business suicide, particularly now his father was ill and Fergus had taken command of the firm. So they promised the man they would determine what the girls were up to and put an end to whatever they were doing.

"Mrs. Johnson, is my wife home?" Zac called, after Fergus had left his office, reassured by their promise to stop them interfering.

Zac had tried Mollie's phone first, but there was no answer. So he called home and put the lady on the loudspeaker so Finley could hear too.

"Yes, sir. She is in the library with Miss Kat, Master Ethan and Master George. They'll be studying for the entire afternoon. Do you need to speak to her?"

"No. That's fine. I just wanted to know if she was there, that's all."

"Any message, sir?"

"No, nothing, thank you. I'll take care of it." Zac rang off.

"Fine, you handle Mollie. And I'll deal with Kat. Ethan, hey?" Finley said with a scowl.

In the last few days, Finley and Kat had devoted every free minute to each other, mainly to lovemaking.

Now they were amorous, the thrill of passion consumed them. They couldn't have enough of each other.

So, when he heard that Ethan was there, it irritated him. Finley knew he had no right to be jealous, since the young man was the girls' study partner and had always been. Still, it didn't sit well with him, not to mention the matching app debacle with Lord Buckley. So neither Finley nor Zac were happy that afternoon. They made their way home to talk to their partners.

There was a knock at the door.

"Come in," said Mollie. Mrs. Johnson came in with the

maid, with a tray of refreshments and cakes for the mid-afternoon break. The maid deposited it on a small table in the library.

"Thank you, Bridget," said Mollie, and the girl left.

The housekeeper poured, knowing already how each one took their tea or coffee, and distributed the cups with many thanks all around.

"Anything else, Mrs. Sorensen?"

"No, thank you, Mrs. Johnson. This is very nice. Tell Mrs. Merton for me, this looks wonderful, too. I'll take it from here," Mollie replied, pointing to the delicious dainty cakes, and the housekeeper nodded and left.

"God, I need this," Kathryn stated. "I am worn out," she said, sipping some tea.

"Me too," echoed George, taking a swig at his coffee and grabbing a cupcake from the tray, wolfing it down in two goes.

"Wow, that cook of yours is amazing. Can you ask her to wrap a few of these cakes to take home?"

"Yes, she's packed a little box for each of you. She is so good, Mrs. Merton, she really is a brilliant cook. She's been with Zac's family for a lifetime. Don't forget to go into the kitchen on your way out to thank her, and she'll give it to you."

"Oh, Mollie, you are a treasure," George said and deposited a kiss on her forehead. "Here, let's put some music on while we have a break, ha? We need to relax for fifteen minutes, or we'll be exhausted by this evening," he went on as he searched for a melody on his phone.

"Oh, I like this music," Mollie said, munching on half a scone with clotted cream and strawberry jam. It was oozing a freshly baked aroma.

"Fuck, this thing is so delicious! Hmm…" Ethan said, eating several small daintily shaped triangles of cucumber sandwiches and a muffin. "Nice to have a cook, hey?"

"Yes, it's nice, she is so sweet to me," Mollie added with a laugh, demolishing the rest of her scone, licking a drop of clotted cream from her fingers.

"Oh, I like this piece of music. Ahh, yes, mambo, I love it," George said as he stood and made a few swaying moves to the tune.

"Mambo?" Mollie stated. She raised her eyebrows, watching him. "Since when do you dance mambo?"

"Ahh, yes, that's Imelda. Bless her. She loves dancing. She is teaching me, you know. I am getting good at it."

They all snorted.

"You non-believers! I tell you, I am good at it." So George extended his arm, offering Mollie his hand. "Come on; let's dance."

"Oh, give over."

"Come on, Mollie. I'll teach you the steps; the basic ones are easy," George urged her.

So Mollie took his hand. After a few basic steps, they started floating around the room to the tune.

"How funny, the two of you dancing mambo." Kathryn laughed while she nibbled at a scone.

"Oh, that's easy. It doesn't look too difficult," Ethan said, following the steps in sync with George and Mollie.

"Would you like to dance, Kat? A bit of movement around the room would do you good. We've been sitting for hours," he stated with a twinkle in his eyes.

Kathryn wasn't sure if it was a good idea, but he poured more tea for her while he was standing.

She took another sip. She realized her friends were enjoying themselves. *Oh, hell, it would be fun,* she thought.

"Well, brace yourself, ladies. Perez Prado, his Orchestra and Mambo No. 5!" George replied swankily, with laughter in his voice and a boom of his hands as he changed to a new song. He slid across the room in a graceful dancing movement as if he were a pro, a real dancer.

George extended his invitation again, "Ready? Your hand, Mrs. Sorensen, please." He bowed, and Mollie chuckled.

She took his hand. She liked to dance, though she had no time for it. She had an inkling she would enjoy it. Zac was an excellent dancer, but he rarely danced, only when he had to. So the fun appealed to Mollie that afternoon.

Ethan did the same and offered his hand to Kathryn. She thought, *what the hell? Why not?*

Music boomed high and mighty in its Latin pulses in the room, the "Mambo No. 5" exploding in vibrant notes, the Cuban rhythms hitting the roof with the Perez Prado orchestra with the swing of a big jazz band style.

They moved in sync to the rhythm, with slight skips and light feet. One, two, three! George taught them the steps, and they all followed him faultlessly.

"Mambo!" they chanted.

The dance flowed round the room, their hips swaying with the eloquence of its dancers.

The piano notes attacked the mambo, while the flute picked up the tempo, the double bass going at it like there was no tomorrow, reflecting the boisterous personality of the Latin rhythms and the four young dancers at hand. Laughter erupted between the young people, as they billowed and swayed to the rhythm, all enjoying the dance.

The music roared in the room. Even Mollie's tiny dog, Peanut, a tan and silver Yorkshire terrier, was hauling with excitement, dashing around, following the dancers up and down the length of the room with great enthusiasm, rushing between them, here and there, and turning a little crazy.

The expanded instrumentation of the band with its many trumpets and saxophones, intermingling with the drums and the double bass, elevated its sexy flow to another level. So did their dancing steps. They swayed to it with much glee doubling out of their lips.

"Mambo, mambo!" they chanted in tune. The characteristic Pérez Prado's deep throat sound bellowed in the room, and the dancers repeated the typical guttural sound on key with the music and a laugh.

"Si, si yo quiero mambo. Mambo... Mambo," George serenaded. They twirled to the melody, moving around the length of the room with light feet, loose shoulders and swaying hips. They all danced with great joy and delight. Bubbling laughter erupted in the room, all in a stylish dance rhythm.

Then, it soon followed another song from the orchestra with a similar arrangement, "Corazon de Melon," and continued on with the melodious voice of Rosemary Clooney booming over in the room.

"Melon, Melon. Corazon de Melon... Melon, Melon," they belted out at the top of their lungs as the brief chorus echoed.

"Your heart is a watermelon heart... just a watermelon heart. Corazon de Melon..." the song said, and they hummed in tune in unison to the song with excitement and amusement, the rhythm making them sway and giggle. The melody, the dance and their beaming smiles enveloped them.

"God. This is fun!" Kathryn said with a fit of giggles, while her ponytail lost its shape, unleashing her locks, her dark, long hair swinging about her in the same fashion as her hips.

They danced like pros.

"Bloody hell, your dancing is remarkable! You learned fast." Ethan reacted with delight in his eyes, making her spin one more time under his arm.

Her hair took center stage in the flow, too, as she loosened up.

"Thank you! These are good dancing feet, and you are not so bad yourself," Kathryn replied with boisterous laughter as she performed another spin, with more swaying of her backside.

He strutted her to the music.

"Well, tonight Mollie's home is the temple of mambo. And you, Kath, are its goddess," Ethan said. His eyes lit up with mischief.

A raucous laugh left their mouths.

"Well, I can see that…" Finley boomed from the doorway with Zac and Mrs. Johnson bearing an amused expression on their faces.

Though Finley, standing tall and mighty, crossed his arms over his chest. His shoulders square, his jaw twitching. He gave Zac a sharp look as he snorted.

"Fin!" Kathryn squealed with delight. "How long have you been standing there?" she asked, halting her dancing.

"Long enough!" he replied with a grunt.

"Oh, don't be a nincompoop, Fin. We were just dancing, having a bit of fun. Remember fun? It's that thing that makes you laugh and have a wonderful time. You should try it some-time; it's good for your health, perfect for the soul! Get your girlfriend to enjoy herself," Mollie said sardonically

Finley lifted an elegant brow at her with a dangerous scowl. He didn't say a word.

Zac gave his wife a severe look, which made her shut her mouth abruptly.

George chuckled and patted Finley on his shoulder. "Why don't you join in the fun?"

"Because I've been working all day, I am damn tired. How about that? I thought you guys were studying. Is this how you study?" he snarled.

"We need to talk, my lovely dancing wife. Now, if you don't mind. This is my library, not Blackpool's Tower Ballroom. So, say goodbye to your friends," Zac said with a deep scowl.

Mollie glanced at him. "But we haven't finished—"

"Oh, yes, you have. Say your goodbyes, dear," Zac drawled.

George raised his eyebrows and looked at Ethan and grimaced. He motioned to the door. So the boys collected their books and papers, said their goodbyes, and Mrs. Johnson saw them out.

They were relieved to be out and far from the glare of the two men. They didn't have a clue what was going on, but the expression on the men's faces wasn't quite friendly, to say the least. Though it didn't stop them from collecting their box of goodies from Mrs. Merton in the kitchen.

"Not so fast, you!" Finley said, gripping Kathryn's wrist as she tried to slip away too, "Not you, love! You stay!" he went on bluntly.

She turned pink and gave him a small smile.

"Now, both of you sit down, please," Zac added, looking at his wife and her friend. "No interruption until I am finished talking, understood?"

Finley released Kathryn's wrist and motioned to a chair. The girls stood there, not moving.

Mollie looked annoyed at her husband. *How dare he dismiss my friends as if I were a naughty child!*

"Sit," Zac growled.

They both fitfully plopped on a chair as their breaths hitched.

"I am not Peanut, you know," Mollie mumbled as she picked up her mischievous dog from the floor, caressing the tiny terrier in her arms. Peanut gave a half-hearted bark at him as if trying to shield her mistress. One look from Zac and even the dog knew to be quiet. So the tiny creature just sat quietly on Mollie's lap, aloof.

But Mollie looked up defiantly. "Zac, I don't understand what's gotten into you, but whatever it is, it was rude to send the boys off like that. I don't think—" she said, ignoring her husband's wish for no interruptions, but a look from him soon shut her up. By now, she knew what that look meant. She was in trouble.

"I swear, one of these days, I am going to kill that fucking boy—" Finley said, but he needn't have mentioned the name, anyway. Everyone understood he was referring to Ethan.

Kathryn gulped. The girls glanced at each other and at their men.

Finley pulled up a chair and reversed it, while he sat astride it, putting his elbows on the back. His eyes were fixed on Kathryn. There were two things bothering Finley. Yes, the issue with Lord Buckley was a thorn in his backside, but the fact she had been dancing sexily with Ethan had blackened his mood beyond redemption.

Zac and Finley exchanged glances, and the latter motioned the other man to start.

Kathryn and Mollie just sat there patiently and let Zac's wrath wash over them. They realized they were at fault, anyhow. It was useless to deny or to make any excuses about what they had done.

In their defense, they said Lord Buckley had been the one to propose them to do it, which was a fact. The old man had insisted on them doing it, pushed them, which was also truth. They were not aware his son had not agreed to it, which was rather questionable.

But the girls enlisted Lord Buckley himself in their defense over the phone. The old fellow confirmed he had asked them to do it. Zac had a hard time convincing the mighty Lord that the girls could not work on this without the express permission of his son. It was his data, and they could not use it without his agreement. Eventually, he got through to him.

So, Zac gave the ladies the benefit of the doubt on this, giving them a warning, "Fine. I'll let it go this time, I know how persuasive the man can be. But you must stop whatever you were doing with pairing Gus with someone in your app, understood? Delete all information and data on him from the app, right now! Is that clear?" Zac said sharply.

"But, Zac, that's a shame. Gus has a perfect pairing! The app has selected his 'top pick,' a great match," Mollie went on, but her husband's irritated expression said it all.

He spelled out that the young aristocrat was not up to this and despised his father's idea, and most of all, he abhorred marriage.

So Mollie promised, reluctantly, that they would remove all references to Fergus on their dating app.

Though Kathryn let Mollie take center stage of their defense, feeling she was best placed to handle her husband's wrath, she was troubled at Finley's silence.

He sat there, straddling his chair, with his eyes in a thin slit and locked on her. Not a sound left his lips, a thin pen in his mouth, like a cigarette. The only item missing was a cowboy hat, and he would have had the same expression of a young Clint Eastwood when he was about to kill a foe in one of his westerns.

It made her gulp. Her mouth went dry.

He kept his eyes fixed on her until she lowered her head and fretted with her hands.

Was he mad at her because of the issue with Lord Buckley or because of her dancing with Ethan? The likelihood, it was both. So she felt uneasy.

It was five days since they'd spent their first night together, and they had been inseparable since then. The hours of love-making had soon brought her up to speed on how to please him and, oh, she had pleased him in every way imaginable. And he made her reach heights of pleasure she didn't know existed. If she had known lovemaking could be this thrilling, this exciting, this pleasurable, she would have acted on it long ago. *Mind you… it is with Finley that sex has become all those things.* She adored the authoritative brute!

So when promises were made and done, Zac was pacified to it, and everyone relaxed. Well, he and Mollie had, as she gave her husband a wanton kiss.

"Are you guys staying for dinner?" he asked, and Kathryn nodded eagerly.

It was not the same for Finley, who darted a sharp glance at her while he handed over a resounding, "No, thank you. We are going."

Kathryn gasped; she knew she was in trouble. She glanced at him, bewildered. "But, Fin, it's better if I stay. Mollie and I haven't finished our studies. You said you are tired; you can go home if you like—" she ventured.

He clasped her arm, pulling her out of the room, while mumbling a curse and his goodnights to his friends over his shoulders.

When they were outside the house, she turned to him furiously. "Oh my God, you are a beast! We are not attached at the hip, you know!" she bellowed at him. "If you must go home, you are free to do so. You have no right to decide things for me, without consulting me," she spat.

"You wanted to stay because you know what's coming, don't you?" He looked at her and raised an eyebrow.

She was hyperventilating, but she had done nothing wrong. She was only dancing. She would not let him get away with his childish behavior every time Ethan was around. "Fine, if this is your attitude, I am going to meet the boys. There!" she replied with a satisfied smile on her lips. Defiant, she crossed her arms on her chest and stared him down.

But he was impassive. "I am going to get the car, then we are going home," he said drily and went over to it.

"No, I said." She launched after him and started walking in the opposite direction. She sent a quick text to George to determine if he was at home or at the pub.

"Pub!"

"Fine, I am coming," she texted back. So, she walked toward the pub instead.

Finley hesitated, not knowing whether to go after her or get the car. He decided he would get the car first and follow her in it. His annoyance redoubled. But the afternoon traffic slowed him down, though from the direction she took, he had an inkling where she was going. Besides, where else would the boys have gone?

When she got to the pub, she glanced in the window to see if she could catch her friends. She saw the boys at a table. George looked up, spotted her and waved. Kathryn waved back.

She was about to go in when a hand came up on her shoulders, gripping her briefly. She looked through the glass window at the reflection of the person behind her, thinking Finley had caught up with her.

But she cried out instead. She screamed at the top of her lungs, then she turned, and there was no one there, though she let out a wail again.

George and Ethan rushed out of the pub when they heard her scream. They found her crouching on the ground in a frenzy.

A sense of foreboding made Finley fly out of his car when he saw the commotion outside the pub. He peeked through the crowd and realized it was Kathryn.

"What the hell happened?" he asked George and Ethan,

who were with her, after he crashed his way through the mass of onlookers, kneeling by her side.

"I don't know. One moment, she was waving at us through the glass front of the pub; the next, she was screaming," George replied, concerned for his friend.

"Please don't crowd her; get people to move away from her," Finley said to him. The young lad moved people along.

"Darling, are you okay?" he asked tenderly, moving her hair out of the way, but she slapped his hand aside.

Then she realized it was him. She couldn't stop shivering. "Oh, Fin. My God." She flung her arms around his neck and sobbed.

"Shush, it's okay, love, I am here," Finley whispered, then he turned to her companions, "George, get her a brandy; let's take her inside. Ethan, please lock my car." Finley launched the keys of his car to the other student. He put an arm around her waist, picked up her up from the ground, and softly drew her inside the pub.

Kathryn was still shivering when she plopped on a chair.

He sat next to her, caressing her hair back. George came back with the brandy.

"Have a few sips, darling, slowly," Finley urged her. She looked at him as if not understanding what he said. "Drink, love, it'll help you," he went on, still caressing her face.

She had a swig of the drink after more shivers, and coughed; she acknowledged him with a small smile.

He had an inkling what she was going to say, but it couldn't be.

"Are you feeling better, my love?" Finley added with the most tender grin he could master. His upset at her dancing shenanigans forgotten, he was worried about her now.

She nodded.

George and Ethan were concerned, too, looking at her,

bewildered. This was a level-headed girl, not prone to screaming for no reason.

"What happened?" Finley glanced at her, then at the boys.

"I was outside, G-George and Ethan w-were inside. I don't know… I smiled, waved at them… oh no, it's too h-horrible," Kathryn stammered and burst out sobbing, her face in her hands.

"Shush, my love, you're fine now. I am here with you," Finley said, smoothing her hair and then taking her palm to his lips.

But she stopped crying abruptly, a harsh expression on her face. "I was waving at them inside, when a hand came over on my shoulders. It squeezed me. For a moment, I thought it was you, but when I looked through the glass window, I saw the reflection. It was him. Him! Oh, dear God!" she blabbered out in one breath.

"Him? Who?" repeated George.

"Professor Blake!" she stated as tears flooded her eyes.

"Professor Blake?" the boys echoed in unison, glancing at each other.

"I swear to you, it was him. Yes, it was!"

"Darling, Peter is dead. He can't harm you," Finley added, bringing her hand to his lips again, but she yanked it out of his hand, staring defiantly at him.

"I tell you, I looked at him. It was him, Peter! There is no mistake this time. He touched my shoulder!" She turned toward George. "You must have seen him from where you were sitting. Didn't you see the person behind me?" she pleaded.

"Yes, I saw her, but with the glaze on the glass, I didn't see the face. Can't be sure; someone was there, though."

"It was him, I tell you, Peter." She sobbed again.

"Wait a minute; did you say *her?*" Finley asked George. "Did you think it was a woman?"

"It was a man, him, Professor Blake. I am not mad," Kathryn cried out. She took another sip of the brandy.

The young lad scratched his head. "Oh, I don't know. There was someone, of that I am sure. I saw the tall figure, the glare, though—"

"But you had the impression it was a girl?"

"Well, I can't tell, maybe… I guess so, oh… I don't know. It was just a second." George was dubious.

"I'm telling you, it wasn't a woman. It was Peter. If you are all against me and don't trust me, I am going home." She rose jerkily and made to move.

"That's okay, darling. I believe you," Finley replied and put his arms around her. "Let's go home, hey?"

She nodded.

The ride home was silent; only Kathryn's occasional sniffs were heard. She still shivered from the shock. She couldn't help it.

Finley's mind was jumping at a hundred miles per second, though. Twice now, she had seen Peter. Once, she had crashed into him in the street, now, outside the pub. This time, he had touched her shoulder. His worry grew rampantly.

Finley didn't believe in ghosts. Peter was dead, buried, and there was nothing that could change that. Though, after what George had said, an insidious suspicion entered his mind. *Or am I certain?*

At home, he looked after Kathryn. He was dedicated to her, devoted. He fed her, yet she had no appetite. Her ordeal had shocked her. He encouraged her to eat. Then he snuggled her in his arms for the evening, caressing her, reassuring her with soothing words until she fell asleep in his arms. He got her shoes off, then her dress, and put her to bed like the most faithful of lovers. It worried him. He knew the girl was no fool, nor impressionable, despite being young.

He understood what she said; Finley had an idea he knew now how this problem had come to life.

He stayed with her for a while, in case she woke up, but she looked fast asleep. So, he wrote her a note, leaving it by the bedside table if she were to wake up.

"Something came up, darling. I'll be back soon! Fin."

He picked up his jacket and car keys and left.

Chapter 11

That night he drove non-stop. He knew how to proceed. A vein twitched in his forehead, realizing someone had hurt his girl. Someone deliberately had set Kathryn up to scare her. Finley had a hunch, though. He would wager his home on it, and he was furious.

It clicked the minute George said, 'Yes, I saw her.' It made sense now.

He made the thirty miles from Oxford to Banbury over the A34 and M40 roads to his destination in forty-five minutes. It had been a long while since he had been on that part of the county.

He parked close by, lingering in his car for a while to get his bearings. He had not been to the house for years, but he knew she was still there.

Finley got out of the car and walked toward the house. A light was showing on the ground floor. He approached her window noiselessly. A cursory inspection inside proved it to him. He recognized her. He moved to the door and went for the buzzer, holding it steady until she opened the door.

"What the—Fin," she said, her voice high-pitched with surprise, wide-eyed, her mouth agape. She wasn't expecting to see him that night, no doubt. She didn't know what to do.

"Hello, Erin," he said with a small smile.

"What do you want?" she spat when she recovered.

"May I come in? Or are you going to leave me out here?"

"It's late, and I don't want to talk to you."

He smiled patiently. He scanned her from top to toe. But it was not a lustful look; it was a warning glare. His green eyes flared the yellow specks in them, and they seemed to flash with fire at her, threatening.

It made her shiver.

"Let me in," he said.

"What the hell are you doing here? It's late," she repeated self-consciously. She shifted on her feet.

"Come on, Erin, you were always bright. Can't you guess?"

"I don't know what you are talking about. And I don't care," she replied. She tried to shut the door on him, but he put a foot in the doorway to stop her.

He pushed the door open with the palm of his hand and, against her will, forced himself inside, closing it behind himself.

Erin backed up a few steps at his entrance. She had always felt somewhat intimidated by him; it was his rugged good-looks that sent her to that place. He scared her and aroused her at the same time. He had that effect on women. She didn't fancy the reason he was there that evening, though. She may have been under stress and grief all these months, but even in the circumstances, she wasn't a fool.

She had an inkling. *Does he know? How? He was nowhere around when I did what I did this afternoon. How could he know? Did the stupid girl tell him? Did he guess? But he would, wouldn't he? Maybe not. Yes, that's it. He is bluffing. He has no proof.*

The turmoil in her mind, with thoughts jamming in her head, and the fear in her soul, made her breath quicken.

Erin had always fancied him, since she first met him years ago, when Finley was at University with her brother.

His manliness attracted her. His rather surly, rugged good looks took her breath away. Sometimes, his brutal, unabashed stares at her made something between her legs flare up. Every time she looked at him, she reverted to those teenage crush markers. Even now, she couldn't avoid it.

At the time, he kept popping up in her X-rated dreams, more than once. She had feared and liked him; she had dreaded and desired him. When he returned from the army, years later, still under the influence of the nightmares that occupied his every sleeping moment, while Erin was engaged to another man, she offered herself to him. Her fantasies became reality.

Finley had not denied her. She was aware of what those clothes were hiding, the most magnificent male specimen she had ever set eyes on. But after a short fling, she had chosen to remain with her then-fiancé over him. She never understood why, *but in hindsight…*

Eventually, she left her fiancé, too, but it was too late to rekindle anything with Finley. He had moved on. That was almost three years ago. She had not seen him again until she saw him with Kathryn in the pub a few days back, when she realized that girl had won the most amazing prize. Him! Finley.

"What do you want, Fin?" She gulped. A thin layer of perspiration erupted on her upper lip.

"Are you not going to offer me something to drink?" he whispered. He wanted her to relax, to encourage her to trust him. Erin was no use to him while she was so highly strung.

He required her to stop doing what she was doing, admit she was wrong. He needed to push her to recognize the misguided path she had undertaken and to amend it. He wasn't sure how she would react, what would happen next, but he needed to protect Kathryn from her.

"Whatever you came here to say, say it and go."

"You know there is something to say then?"

"Know? I don't have the foggiest! Leave me alone! Go away." Her mind started going into turmoil. She was terrified and humiliated, affronted. She wanted to punish him, but she was glad he was there. Her brain was in a whirlwind of frenzy. She had to push these thoughts out of her head. The man, himself, was there in her presence, and by the determined expression on his face, he meant business. She required all her wits about her.

"Come on, Erin, you know!"

"It's late, and I have no wish to talk to you."

"Leave Kathryn alone. I am warning you."

"Kathryn? Who the hell is she?"

"You know very well who she is and what you're doing to her. Kathryn is my girlfriend. This must stop, now. Understood?"

"Leave, do you hear me?" She turned to go to the door, but he grabbed her wrist.

She slapped his hand. "What the hell do you think you are doing? Let me go."

"Erin, listen to me. You have your entire future ahead of you. Whatever this is, don't let it ruin your life. Leave Kathryn alone. I love her," he said in a gentle whisper. He let her hand drop.

She stared at him. "Go away," she whispered.

"Why are you doing this? To avenge your brother? Or are you doing this because of me, hey? Because Kathryn is with me? I don't want to know. No, I don't need an answer. But this must stop right now. It can only finish one way. Do you hear? Don't let it end with you going to prison, or worse, the same way as Peter."

She slapped his face with all her might, moved to the door, and opened it. "Get out! Now, Fin, before I call the police."

"I am warning you, you hurt one hair on Kathryn, or scare her again, I swear, this will end in tears for you. Leave her alone. I am not telling you again." He was out of the door which banged shut behind him.

The moment he left, perspiration erupted on her forehead. She wiped it with her hand. She felt faint, her legs weak. Erin whimpered a sound of terror, the one she had contained during his visit. Her heart was thundering in her chest. It amazed her that he had not heard it thumping, ready to explode.

She flopped on her settee and struggled to calm herself. Surprised, she realized she was massaging the wrist he had touched. Having seen him after so long, a question popped up in her mind. *Is he right; am I fooling myself?* Did she start this silly plan because of Peter's death or the fact the girl had him now, because Kathryn had Finley?

Could it be she was deceiving herself, and this had nothing to do with her brother's death? What was the truth? *No, no, no!* She denied it. *Peter is the reason, the truth. They killed him! That's the fact. This is to avenge my brother!* The reason she had done what she did. Was it not? Yet, her cheeks burned. Was she deluding herself? But she insisted on it. She repeated it, time and time again, like a mantra. She tried to convince herself.

Why not start with Mollie or Zac, then? Why did you choose Kathryn instead? her inner voice admonished her.

She'd studied the girl that first night, but she hadn't concocted her revengeful plan until she saw Finley with Kathryn, until she realized Finley had feelings for the girl. It was the last straw that carried her over the edge, over and above her unending sorrow.

Could Finley be right? And she was just vulgarly jealous? Like her brother had been jealous of Zac's life and riches. No, no, no! It was impossible! She didn't care for Finley, not after all these years. Why would she? She hadn't thought about him for years, so why now?

Maybe it irked her seeing them happy. That was it! Perhaps this was the reason. They were fortunate. They had found love, while she was grieving, and her life was only infinite grief and sadness, torture.

Oh, dear Lord! It confused her. Finley was trying to confuse her too, now.

Erin got up and went to the sideboard. She poured a brandy to calm herself, and downed it in two long gulps. She crumpled back onto the sofa, pulling her legs to her body, and wrapping her arms around them. She rocked herself on the spot, muttering to herself.

"How could I let this go so far?" she mumbled as she shivered. *What the hell is going on in my mind,* she wondered. *Am I crazy?*

She needed help! She realized she was on the verge of collapse, of mental collapse.

Erin had always been the sensible twin, trying to put her brother on the straight and narrow. *Look at me now...*

Why did she turn into this dark, dangerous woman? It was not like her. She was not this... no! Her game seemed childish and petty now. Astonished, she realized she didn't like it, not really, not anymore. Finley's presence had been like a slap in the face, a wakeup call.

She understood she didn't enjoy her plan after all. Finley had raised her from a deep, dark nightmare and brought her back to reality. But would she be able to stop this madness? She didn't know.

She had become a weak, pathetic human being; her usual self was strong-minded and willful. But unwavering grief did weird things to people. She sobbed uncontrollably, long and hard. God! What was she going to do? She slumped into a frenzy.

Though she had not admitted to anything, Finley had figured it out...

He knew!

Sweet Jesus, I am in trouble!

Chapter 12

A few days had passed since that incident, yet it seemed, rather abruptly, Kathryn had dismissed the problem. She didn't look upset any longer. She stopped talking about the matter, at least to Finley. Even when he asked her about it, she appeared to dislike the conversation and soon changed topics.

Finley realized she'd had a tremendous shock, thinking it was Peter, and though he knew better now, he wouldn't force the issue. It would be in her own good time.

She was still persuaded she had seen Peter, but it didn't seem to drop her into a frenzy of anxiety anymore. She returned to her customary self-composure.

Finley was glad, but something made him uneasy. He couldn't pinpoint the reason, but he was. He had a sixth sense for these things; that's why he had been a great soldier, a brilliant strategist. Though he had no proof, he knew the truth.

He was certain Erin had concocted the deception. He thought best to keep it to himself, at least for now. There was no point in upsetting Kathryn again by telling her. So, he didn't. He shared his concerns and the result of his visit to Erin only with Zac, who had the same suspicions.

So, they agreed to be vigilant and keep Erin under observation. If she made another move, they wouldn't be so lenient with her. They hoped Finley's warning would be an ample deterrent to stop Erin's foolishness. Notwithstanding, she had not admitted to anything.

Finley was keeping a close eye on Kathryn, too. He would not let her out of his sight unless someone else was with her. He worried about her, so much so, that he had even abandoned any potential rebuke on her dance with Ethan. Finley had dismissed the dance as a young girl's high spirits. He had been gentle, loving with her instead.

That evening after dinner, he was kissing her on the settee. They were in her home in the living room with her housemates out of the way at an all-night party. He thought he was about to bless Kathryn's own bed for the first time with their lovemaking.

They had spent most of their evenings together in his apartment in his bed, rather than in her house with two housemates, where privacy was at a premium. So, he had high hopes for the night to try hers, too.

But at around nine, the girl became tense, and a kind of veiled uneasiness descended on her. Finley was unsure what had suddenly triggered Kathryn's change of demeanor. She glanced at her wristwatch discreetly, trying to be inconspicuous about it. But he didn't miss her furtive glances at her watch several times.

She looks impatient, restless, he thought.

Kathryn seemed a scant agitated and aloof. Not even his kisses or his caresses, which usually sent her into a delirium of desire, were doing it for her.

"Are you okay, Kat? You look a slight… distracted, this

evening," Finley said with a wrinkled brow and a grin on his face. Yet the smile was fake.

"Distracted? Why, no!" she replied, blushing violently. "It's just that I have been studying hard today, with lessons and that, you know. I am tired. I have a headache, not feeling myself. Nothing that a good night's sleep won't cure, though," she blurted out in one go, her blush intensified.

She got up, paced for a moment, and looked at her wrist-watch again, nonchalantly. She gave him a brief smile which seemed to say, *"You are lovely, but tonight, you would be adorable if you left."*

He smiled back, rose and reached for her. He kissed her. "Sure, you're right. I'll leave you alone tonight. You go up to bed, have a goodnight's sleep. You'll feel better in the morning," he replied, stroking her face softly.

She smiled, and it seemed to him, her grin said, *Thank God!* He didn't miss the small intake of breath, of relief, either.

"Are you sure you don't mind?" she added, almost as an afterthought, with a genuine apologetic smile.

He caressed her hair back, giving her a goodbye kiss. "I'll survive a night without you. Mind you, don't make a habit of this," he said gingerly.

She sighed with contentment, and he left her house.

Finley had been in the Army Intelligence Corps long enough to understand when someone was lying. Kathryn was fibbing, but why? He was convinced she had no headache. She just wanted him out of her way. *What's she up to?*

So, he got into his car, started it, and drove along the road, as she looked out her window and waved. But he only parked it farther up the street, out of sight from her, and waited.

It intrigued him, so he hung around and watched. Was his hunch right? Did she want him out of her home?

What's the little minx doing? Hmm… what's going on? He promised himself he would wait half an hour, in case he was wrong, then go home.

In fact, he only had to wait ten minutes, when he saw Mollie's red battered mini arrive.

The woman was so fond of her mini that not even a present from Zac, a brand new sports car, had made her change her favoritism toward her old car, which she was now parking in front of Kathryn's house… the parking space Finley had just left.

I knew it!

Mollie got out of the vehicle in her flowery dress under a loose red wrap. Kathryn opened the door immediately to her, before she reached it, as if she was expecting her.

It shocked him. Finley remained there, musing on this. If his girl wanted to spend an evening with her friend, she should have said so. Surely, he was not such a despot that she could not confide such a wish to him. A sudden rush of shame ate at him. Perhaps Kathryn was right, and he was a controlling brute, too authoritarian. But he didn't want secrets between them.

He mused for a while in his car, sitting there, his thoughts on his overbearing behavior with her. Another surge of guilt filled him. He scratched his forehead and rubbed a hand over his face. A tightening in his chest constricted him. *How could I do this to her? Moron,* he told himself.

Kathryn was young and sweet, and he had made her feel uneasy in talking about what she wanted. This was his fault. He should be more lenient with her. He had been too severe with her, and the girl felt she could not point out to him she yearned to see a friend.

He would let her be for tonight. Tomorrow, he would

130

explain to her, she was free to spend time with Mollie or any friend whenever she wished. She shouldn't be coy to tell him. She didn't have to hide her wishes from him.

It was fine for him to share her with her friends. He didn't mind it at all... *perhaps a bit, and only with that stupid boy, Ethan.* He mused, perhaps she didn't want to upset him. *Ah, the charming girl.* He smiled to himself.

Yes, that was it. *She won't upset me or hurt my feelings, by wanting to spend time with her friend rather than me. The girl is like honey! I adore the saucy minx.*

After about ten minutes of musings, he laughed, proud of her tender sensibilities. But he would address the issue in the morning.

He was about to start the car and drive home, when Kathryn's front door opened again. He saw two figures walk out of the house toward Mollie's car. The two characters were dressed all in black from head to toe. Black hoodies, black slacks, and other black paraphernalia covered them.

He wouldn't have recognized the girls if he hadn't been well acquainted with them. As it was, he recognized the pair. Mollie's tall and willowy figure was unmistakable, as was Kathryn's buxom and sinuous frame. If he hadn't known them so well, and they weren't coming out of her house, he wouldn't have looked at them once, let alone recognized them. But he knew better!

Mollie had changed into a black outfit. So had Kathryn. From her dainty, feminine skirt and pink camisole she was wearing earlier on, she had changed into black slacks, a black hoodie and a black scarf. Not even her hair was visible under the hood.

What the hell! What are they up to?

Stupid me... feeling guilty, thinking it was me... He shook his head, his nostrils flaring. Irritation gripped him. Oh, she was in trouble, now!

He leaned back in his seat, inhaled deeply for a few seconds, watching them get into the car. Suddenly, dread replaced annoyance soon enough. He dragged the palms of his hands over the steering wheel, and a shudder took hold of him. A sense of foreboding didn't sit well with him. *What the hell?*

Finley was stunned, though it intrigued him, the trouble-makers. The two lovelies from hell wanted him out of the way. They were now out of the house, dressed like cat burglars ready for business. *They were up to no good, no doubt!* Dread transformed itself, once more, back into irritation and annoyance.

The girls got into Mollie's car and drove off. He put his car into gear and followed them. They embarked on the road out of Oxford toward the A34, empty at that time of the night. When they joined the M40, he understood where they were heading.

"Is Mollie going somewhere tonight?" Finley asked Zac over his mobile phone while driving behind them at a distance.

"Yes, why? She left about an hour ago. She is going to her mother in Devon, back tomorrow, why?"

"Is Kathryn traveling with her?" he urged, in case he was mistaken, and they were heading the long way around, but he wasn't wrong. Besides, they would not go to her mom dressed like burglars.

"No. Not that I know of. Why? What's the matter?"

So, Finley told him where the girls were at that precise moment, and his suspicions as to where they were headed instead.

Zac ranted, cursed and wanted to join him, but Finley calmed him down. "Don't worry. Stay home; you may be of more use there. We won't know just yet, but I'll bring them back. Though I have to find out their intentions first."

"I still feel we should've told them, in case something happens, so they know where we are," Kathryn said when they were nearing the outskirts of town. The sensible girl was not completely at ease.

"Tell them? Are you mad? They wouldn't approve. They would never allow it! God, you know how they are. Do you expect we would be here now if they knew? On the road to Banbury? Not on your life! Have you understood nothing about these two men?"

"No, I suppose you're right. Finley would have kittens if he knew."

"Zac would turn my ass scarlet! I'll tell you that," Mollie scoffed.

"He would? Does he…" Kathryn didn't want to pry, brandishing a hand in the air, and her friend laughed.

"Oh, Kat, sometimes I think you are like an innocent child." Mollie snorted in an unladylike manner. Her companion joined her with a giggle, then they laughed whole heartedly.

Mollie told her the things she liked to do with her husband in bed… which was an eye opener for the girl.

Yet Kathryn had been an accomplished pupil for Finley, a quick learner, and she caught up fast. Not to mention the spanking that had sent her into a delirious wave of pleasure that first night. Kathryn had loved him smacking her backside, and he had humored her eagerly again. So, she agreed perfectly with Mollie on that score.

"Right, we are almost there, sweetie! Now, we must be careful. Tonight is purely reconnaissance to learn what's going on. We stop on the green for a few minutes to survey the area. Then we go near the house to see what's what, and we agree what to do next. Did you get the knife?" Mollie said, parking the car somewhere around the corner form Erin's house.

RAFFAELLA ROWELL

"Yes, I did. He doesn't realize I've taken it, though. What if he finds out?"

"But he won't, will he? Unless you tell him. Like Zac won't find out I have picked up his handgun."

"His gun? Jesus, Mollie! Have you lost your mind? Why do you need a gun, anyway, if we are only doing reconnaissance? We won't barge into the woman's house tonight, will we?"

"No, not tonight. Hell, I'm not sure what we are going to do. We must see if she is alone first, how it all looks, how it all works around there. But I heard Finley say that even during reconnaissance missions, the military is always armed."

"Bloody hell, Mollie, we are not soldiers. And this isn't an army mission, is it?"

"Oh, sweet Jesus, Kat, stop that. We have them now, so don't fuss. Let's get used to them in case we should need them."

"Good God, you don't intend to shoot the woman, do you?"

"No, of course not. It's for protection. If that woman is trying to scare the hell out of you, making out she is her dead brother, then she is crazy, like her brother, like Peter was! God knows what she has planned. Believe me, we need this to protect ourselves. Remember, I know what Peter was capable of, and you also suffered firsthand at his violence. God, Kath, I still have nightmares about Antibes. And the man turned you black and blue with bruises when he hit you then, too. You still have the scar on your forehead from the fall, have you forgotten? Peter threw you down the stairs, as a warning to me, for the sheer pleasure of it and to show me he was serious about his threats to Zac. Peter had a wretched, treacherous plan. He was a cunning, bad man. He almost killed Zac, and if I had not done what I did first, he would have killed him. I tremble every time I think of it. Do you think it doesn't haunt me? Oh, how it does, I tell you! And this is his sister we are talking

134

about. His twin! And by the looks of it, just as devilish. She is evil, doing this. I am taking no chances," Mollie urged.

Kathryn gulped and cast her mind back at that frightful day in Antibes, when she was in the hospital suffering from the aftermath of her fall down the stairs. To make matters worse, Peter had attacked her again after she revealed he had been Mollie's ex-lover.

She shivered at the memory, closed her eyes, and tried to put it out of her mind. But her companion soon brought her back to the moment.

Mollie rummaged in her handbag and fished out the hand-gun. She waved it at her to show it off.

"Jesus, Mollie, stop waving that thing at me!"

"Let me see the knife," Mollie replied.

Kathryn searched in her backpack. "Here, it has a gorgeous handle, doesn't it?"

"Umm, never seen this knife before, is it new?" Mollie said, giving it a quick glance, but her phone rang, the sound making them jump.

"Jesus, bloody hell! What is that?" Kathryn said with a hand on her heart, steadying herself, inhaling and exhaling.

"Don't worry; it's my phone. Oh, damn, it's Zac! Be quiet, and don't say a word. I've got to take this," she said, pointing at the car phone holder.

"Oh, darling! Hi, how are you?"

"Are you home yet? How's your mother?" Zac asked sharply.

"No, not yet, darling! Still driving," she said, lying. *"I'll call you when I get there. Not long now, I promise. Let's talk later."*

"Sure! You do that."

"Bye, darling."

. . .

"Shit! He'd have a fit if he knew," Mollie said after the call, taking a deep breath. She was a tad worried, in case he should find out about her escapade, but soon dismissed it.

"He sounded in a foul humor."

"He's always in a dreadful mood when I leave," she said with a giggle. "So, show me the knife. Is it new?" Mollie went on.

"Who knows? Fin has a gorgeous polished oak casket. The inside is covered in smooth red velvet, and it has a few knives in it, all laid out in a lovely way, with exquisite, intricately carved handles. They must be very expensive. That's where I got this one. I hope he won't miss it tonight. He thinks I don't know he has them. He's never shown them to me." Kath sighed.

"Oh, been rummaging through his flat, have you? Behind his back, ha! You minx," Mollie added with an uncouth laugh.

"Well, I was curious. He can be so mysterious sometimes." Kat giggled, and they laughed together.

"Okay, enough chit chat. Ready?" Mollie said.

Kath gulped but nodded. She smoothed her hands down the front of her slacks, her palms sweaty with apprehension. She didn't know what to expect. "Right! Let's go."

The girls made their way out of the car and turned the corner, which brought them onto a small green in the large square. The green was about thirty meters from Erin's house. They settled behind a gigantic tree on the green.

"What now?"

"Well, hmm, look around, in case you can pick up things. Be observant," Mollie said, crouching behind the tree and raising her neck to peer at the house.

"What things? Observant of what?"

"Hell, what do I know? Use your initiative," she said, and her companion giggled.

"Shush, quiet!"

Finley parked the car at a short distance from them and waited. The girls were still in the car.

"Zac? We are in Banbury now. Call whoever is watching Erin's house for us, so he knows we're here, and tell him not to bother us. I'll handle this."

"What the hell are they doing? I called the bloody chit, and she said she was still driving to her mother. The little monkey! Wait until I get my hands on her!" Zac said in annoyance.

Finley snorted. "They are in the car," he said with a laugh.

"What the hell is so funny?"

"Nothing, really, but you've got to grant it to them. They figured it out by themselves."

"Those two are troublemakers. I'll tell you, I bet this was Mollie's idea. She knew Peter had a twin from way back. It must have been easier for her to put two and two together when George mentioned he thought he had seen a woman behind Kath outside the pub, when the woman scared her."

"Jesus, they are fearless! Oh, wait, they are coming out of the car. Speak to you later, bro! I am going after them."

"Fin, don't let them get into danger; just stop this nonsense right now. Bring them home."

"Oh, yea! Sure. Will do." Finley waited for the girls to step ahead, and then he came out of the car to follow them. He was curious and wanted to know what they were going to do next. He followed them, perching himself behind a bush.

When they hovered behind a tree for ten minutes, doing nothing, it was obvious to him they didn't know what to do. It was clear they had no plan other than to see if Erin lived there.

He smiled to himself and shook his head in disbelief. Time to stop this charade! So, he made his way to them.

"Which one is hers, did you say?" asked Kathryn, stretching her neck to get a good view of the houses on the other side of the green.

"Number 32, end of terrace, with the black door and stained windows. Right in your line of sight." Mollie pointed in the general direction.

"Do you think we should make our way toward the house then, to see what's going on inside?" Kathryn said, "Everything seems quiet out here, anyway. What do you think?"

"And I say, no, absolutely, not! You are not going anywhere," Finley replied. His voice sounded polite, calm but firm, and peremptory behind them, all the more chilling because it was all those things.

It made the ladies jump out of their skin with a gasp.

"Fin!" Kathryn shrieked as she spun to him. Her eyes wide, she blanched.

"Jesus, you scared the life out of me! Don't creep up on me like that again," Mollie said, turning, holding her revolver and waving it.

"For crying out loud, a gun? Are you out of your mind? Give me that, slowly." He opened his palm. She made no movement to dispense with it. "Now, Mollie, give it to me!" He sounded as calm and as chilly as the polar caps.

She sighed and placed the gun in his hand, rolling her eyes.

He inspected it, then gave them a fierce look, his face in a scowl.

"For God's sake, I could have shot you, creeping up on us like that," she whimpered.

"Yes, you could have if you'd cared to take the security catch off."

"Security catch?" Mollie asked with a wrinkled brow.

"Does Zac know you have his gun? No, wait, stupid question. I can guess…" he said ironically and then turning to his girlfriend, added,"…and you, young lady, give me whatever you are hiding behind your back."

Kathryn shifted from foot to foot. She swallowed.

"Give it to me. *Now!*" he urged her.

Even in the night's blackness, she could see the yellow freckles in his green eyes spitting fire at her. And, again, if it weren't for the dark, inky night, she would have seen a vein twitch in his forehead, too. She pushed her palm out with it.

He glanced at her hand and freed her of the knife, then he inspected it. If he had recognized it as his, he didn't show it, revealing nothing. But the fierce look on his face said it all. "Let's get back home before anything stupid happens. Stop this nonsense. We'll talk later about how much trouble you are both in."

"No!" Kathryn cried out, and two sets of eyes stared at her.

Finley was shocked. "What did you say? No?" he echoed, yet he had heard her perfectly. He lifted an eyebrow.

It amazed even Mollie.

"I said, *no!*" Kathryn repeated, raised her chin to him in total defiance.

"Our plan was to talk to that woman, to make her change her ways, to end this preposterous thing of hers. We wouldn't talk to her tonight, granted. This was only reconnaissance. But now that I am here, now that I've come this far, that's what I am going to do! I am not leaving until I do, and if you stop me, Fin, I warn you, I'll scream my head off until the police come," Kathryn said with a defiant expression in her eyes.

It astonished Finley, Mollie too. They looked at her, speechless.

"Oh, dear! She's got that crazy look in her eyes, Fin. She means it," Mollie suggested.

"Kath, we are going home. Please." he repeated in a more appeasing tone and sighed, but his expression was one that said, *God, don't let my patience desert me!*

But she turned and started walking toward the house.

"Mollie, stop him if he follows me," Kathryn said over her shoulders, then she burst into a run.

Finley stood there astonished for a moment, then he tried to run after her. But Mollie seized his arm, struggling to hold him, slowing him down. He tried to shake her off, but she grasped his other arm too. They wrestled for a few more seconds until Finley shook her off him. He checked she was unharmed, then he rushed off after Kathryn.

The delay in Mollie tampering with his chase gave Kathryn enough time to reach the house. She thumped on the door hard. "Erin, open up. Come on; I need to talk to you," she bellowed and thumped louder.

Erin opened. "What the hell—" Her face blanched at seeing the girl.

"May I come in?" Kathryn said calmly, giving a sigh of relief. Without waiting for a reply, she pushed in.

Erin hesitated, then she stepped aside to let her in unchallenged. She was about to close the door behind her when a foot blocked her from doing so.

He pushed the door gently open.

She gasped. "Fin!" she said in astonishment.

He made his way into the house, too.

Erin looked from Kathryn to Finley. She didn't know what to make of their sudden arrival so late that night. But it didn't bode well, whatever their intentions. She was about to close the door, when Mollie pushed it wide with her hands.

"Jesus, what is this? A procession? What the hell is she doing here?" Erin snapped, pointing at Mollie, and not thrilled at having her home invaded by her ex-lover, his new lover and her brother's murderous, infamous ex-girlfriend. The last thing in the world she wished to do was to talk to them, and all at once, ganging up on her. So Erin felt nervous and anxious.

She clasped the sides of her dress several times. "What do you want? And make it quick before I scream," she said with a scowl, the furious biting of her lower lip betraying her anxiety. She tried to look tough. Erin was a tall woman by any standards. She towered above the two younger girls, but they didn't seem intimidated.

Finley was about to reply something, but Kathryn put her hand up to him to shut him up. His mouth closed abruptly in dismay. The hint of exasperation in his eyes couldn't be contained. *I hope she doesn't make a habit of this!* Though, within him, he was proud of her for being fearless, for taking the bull by the horns, so to speak.

"I want you to stop doing whatever you are doing to me. It isn't healthy, and it's wrong. And before you deny it, don't bother. I know it's you. Everyone knows you are a make-up expert, and your brother looked so much like you. This game of yours has to stop now. Or I'll go to the police, understood? I swear, I will. Please. How long before the police would find things in your home to prove it is you, hey? Do you want to go to prison?" Kathryn spoke in a rush.

"I don't know what the hell you are talking about. Now leave! Get out of my house."

"Erin, please, you need help. You must see a doctor. Don't deny this. We know it's you. You can't scare me anymore. Your little game is over, anyway. I am well aware you have suffered, but this has to stop! I am not at fault for what happened to your brother," Kathryn pleaded.

"She's right. We won't call the police, but you must see a doctor. You are not yourself. You're not like Peter. I know a good clinic. They have good doctors there, and they can help you get over this. You've been under enormous stress in the last few months. Please, Erin," Finley beseeched with a softness in his voice.

"I said, get out of my house! I don't need any help. How dare you come into my house and shoot these wild accusations at me? Get out!" Erin said through clenched teeth, taking a step back with fearful eyes. But deep down, she realized it was all true. She needed help! And soon, before things got out of hand. She stumbled on her feet, turning here and there, biting her lip furiously in anxiety, figuring out what to do next. But she was with her back against the wall. She had no way out.

Besides, she'd gotten awfully alarmed at her own unpredictable actions, her erratic behavior. Since Finley's previous visit, she had become more agitated, questioning her atrocious exploits. Though she would never admit to it, she was glad for the showdown but fearful of it, too, at the probable outcome. She wanted to stop herself from doing what she was doing, but she couldn't see how she would do it.

"Erin, you are still grieving for your brother and your parents. Grief does strange things to people, but I couldn't help it. I still have nightmares for what I did in Antibes. It wasn't easy, but I got help to see me through this. Please forgive me! Peter was about to kill Zac. He shot him twice. He was going to do it again, to finish him off. Believe me, he gave me no choice. But you must stop this. You are not like him, I know you're not! It will end up badly; someone can get hurt. Please," Mollie begged.

"You bitch! Get out of my house!" Erin said with vehemence. Mollie's words angered her, still refusing to believe it, but in her heart of hearts, she realized Mollie had said the truth. Erin knew her brother well enough to figure out each word the girl said was true. Besides, the case files had confirmed the same. So she fretted. Perspiration erupted on her upper lip. Her heart thundered in her chest, ready to explode.

They were at an impasse, and silence descended for about a minute. They were all guarded.

Erin paced, looking at each one, not daring to hold their stare, unable to say a word. She was agonizing, her own arms wrapped against her stomach protectively. She was on the verge of collapse.

They fixed their eyes on her, expectantly, until Finley broke the deadlock. "I'll give you ten minutes to consider this. We'll be outside. Pack some clothes, and I'll take you to the clinic myself, tonight. The senior doctor is a friend, and I'll put in a special word for you. Please do it, for all our sakes, but mainly for yours. You need support. I promise we won't press charges if you do. You must seek help and do it now. Stop this nonsense. And don't think of running away. You know how that ended for your brother. You are young, beautiful and clever; move on with your life. You deserve a good life," Finley replied, his words gentle, but there was no doubting the firmness of his statements and his veiled threat. He paused and looked at her.

Erin was fidgeting with her hands on her dress. Tears started flowing down her cheeks. She wiped them and glared at him. There was no animosity in her eyes, he discovered in surprise. Only expectancy, pleading eyes, perhaps even trust, but Erin said nothing while tears continued to flow.

"Girls, let's go. Let's wait outside while she makes up her mind. Ten minutes, Erin, and pack a bag," he repeated.

The ladies looked at each other dubiously, but they moved out with him.

"She'll run away," Mollie said, the moment they were back on the green.

"No, she can't. She has nowhere to go."

"What if she decides not to come with us tonight? Are we

pressing charges if she doesn't cooperate? The girl needs support; she is under a lot of stress. We won't help her if we call the police, but we can't leave things as they are, either. What are we going to do?" Kathryn asked.

"We'll just have to wait and see, won't we?" he said calmly. He called his friend at home.

"Zac, call Dr. Stewart. We are taking Erin to him tonight. She needs help. And get young Goran; he is going with her. She'll need someone to look after her for a while, even at the clinic, whether or not she likes it. At least until the doctor tells me she is okay and we can trust her. I am not taking any chances, even if she agrees to go to the clinic. Make sure Goran is at your house by the time we are back," Finley said, and he explained what he had in mind.

He was getting ahead of himself, given the lady had decided nothing yet.

"What if she doesn't agree?" Kathryn asked. "Isn't your call a tad premature?"

"What choice does she have? She has no option. We'll wait."

They paced outside her house relentlessly. Ten minutes had now passed. There was no sign of Erin.

"Perhaps we should go back in, plead with her, make her understand this is the best choice for her. She needs help. She can't go on doing these preposterous things. What she was doing to me was not healthy," Kathryn suggested. She was concerned and continued pacing.

"What are we going do? She won't agree," Mollie said later. "We've waited over twenty minutes now. What if she's run away?"

Then they heard a noise, and they turned. The door opened, and Erin came out. Her eyes were downcast, and she was still fidgeting with her dress with one hand. In the other, she had a big bag.

They all smiled at her and sighed with relief.

Kathryn ran to her, took her bag and patted her tenderly on the back. "It'll be all right, Erin, you'll see, I am sure of it. You have been through a lot in such a short time. You'll be fine," she said with a comforting smile.

Finley grabbed the bag from his girlfriend, then he looked at the tall woman. "I promise, I'll look after you. You'll be fine. Time to go now," he said soothingly. He took her hand and squeezed it.

"Give me your house keys. I'll lock the door," Mollie said, smiling.

"Come on, Erin, you get in my car. Mollie, you drive with Kath. I'll be behind you all the way."

So the party moved on, and they returned to Oxford.

———

The drive was rather silent in both cars, given each passenger was ruminating on the events of the night. Though they were happy with the outcome, it had been a torturous expedition.

Even Erin, deep down, was delighted she had taken steps to get herself out of the mess and dreadful events she had steered herself into, at least she hoped so. Perhaps Finley was right, and the medical team would support her, help her out of it. She had to try. Nonetheless, she was apprehensive. She didn't know what to expect.

Finley couldn't help thinking, although they had been successful tonight, Kathryn had put herself in danger on such a foolish mission. She had no means of telling it would produce a peaceful result, no idea of what might have happened. For all he knew, Erin could have been violent toward her.

Not only that, the chits had gone on this wild goose chase armed to the teeth. *A handgun and knife, for goodness' sake, reckless and disconcerting. Even by their standards.*

On one hand, it caused him to laugh, thinking of their fearless and cocky undertaking, but on the other, it made his blood steam in irritation at the unruliness and danger the ladies had exposed themselves to on that night. These girls were mischievous, lionhearted and bold, make no mistake, but oh, so reckless. If he was going for Kathryn as his woman, as he surely was, he had a battle on his hands. He realized it now. On the surface, she was sweet, and she was like honey to him, but at times, her steely determination and bravado made her indomitable and fearless. She was a kitten, with long, sharp nails and no fear of using them if the moment called for it. He liked that in her, but it also worried him. He would have to deal with her later and explain a few more rules to her. *Or perhaps in the morning. Tonight, the other lady was the priority.*

In fact, Finley did have another girl to worry about now, Erin. He had promised her he would look after her, to see her well again. From tonight, this lady was now under his protection, too. He had silently assumed responsibility for this girl, as a friend, in her hour of need. To ensure she got better, he couldn't just wash his hands of her. Though not exactly a girl, Erin was a grown woman, a thirty-three-year-old woman. They were the same age. So he hoped the clinic and the doctors would work their magic and restore her into a stable human being again, out of her torment. Thus, he could relinquish his duty sometime soon. He would have his hands full with Kathryn as it was, so the sooner Erin went back to her former self, the better.

Bloody hell! He would have his job cut out! Thank God, at least Mollie was off his hands. She was Zac's concern, and his friend could deal with his own wife. *Small mercy! Women!*

The drive had been comparatively uneventful. So, after they reached Oxford, they got out of their cars and into Zac's house.

Mollie directed them to the sitting room and asked them to make themselves comfortable. With her back to the door, she turned when she heard footsteps behind her, as Zac came into the room with a young man. She peeked at her husband, fully aware of the fact that, not merely had she lied to him about where she was going, but she had taken his gun without permission and gone into a dangerous situation of which he would never approve. *Jesus, I'm in trouble!*

The moment Zac saw her, his face told her the full story. She was more than in trouble.

I am beyond trouble. I am heading for the rocks!

His eyes flashed a warning at her that said, *don't say a word! I don't want to hear it!* She knew that look well, the exasperation behind it, too.

Mollie gave him a small smile, but to no avail.

A frustrated shake of his head said to her, *don't even try! Don't you dare!* And when he was close enough to her, he dropped his lips to her ear and said, "I'll deal with you later. First things first!"

It was a steady, calm murmur, so calm that it made her gasp. It chilled her.

He took her arm, gently but firmly, and pulled her out the door. "Ask Mrs. Johnson to bring in some refreshment, then you and Kath can go up to bed. We must talk to Erin in private. We need to make some arrangements. Off you go, both of you." He darted a glance at Kathryn too, who lowered her eyes and fiddled with the sleeves of her hoodie, then looked up at Finley. The latter only raised an elegant brow at her, nodded his approval of Zac's dictum, then gave her an abrupt sway of his head to the door.

She winced.

"We s-should stay t-too," Mollie replied with a stammer, but when Zac dipped his head toward her and flashed his usually mellow, sultry, honey-colored eyes with a fierce light, taking a breath in and flaring his nostrils, she knew she had gone too far. She bit her bottom lip, tugged at her hair furiously, signaled to Kath to follow her, and they darted from the room in a jiffy.

Zac motioned to Erin to sit on the sofa, and he sat opposite her in the matching armchair. "Glad you came," he said to her with a sincere smile. "I've planned for you to stay at Doctor Stewart's clinic. He is a friend, a skilled doctor. His clinic is in the Cotswolds, in a lovely spot in the countryside, in Worcestershire. The medical team is first class, and I'm sure you'll be comfortable there."

She lowered her eyes, not daring to look at him, embarrassed at what she had done. Erin didn't venture to say a word. She had a way of assessing situations quickly.

Zac and Mollie were a loving couple, Erin would wager her car on it. Even after having seen them in action for only two minutes, and not in a particularly peaceful moment, it seemed to her they could understand each other with just a glance.

She sighed, missing that closeness with someone special who could make her feel alive.

But Zac brought her back into the room from her musings. "Erin?"

She bowed her consent.

"Dr. Stewart's medical unit will give you all the support you require and will treat you well. You'll soon feel stronger and back to your old self. I don't envisage you staying there long, but you must want to get better. You went through a lot of stress and grief, and these things, sometimes, can push people to do unpredictable things," he stated with an intimate and tender voice.

It surprised her he should sound so gentle with her after what she had done, after what her brother had done to him, but Zac seemed so sincere, and she was glad of it.

"You must cooperate with the doctors for the treatment to achieve results," he said, but he added this in a sterner tone, which left her no doubt he meant business.

She raised her head to him, looking into his eyes. Guilt abruptly flashed through her at what Peter had done to him. After all these months, suddenly, she was too ridden with guilt at her twin's appalling behavior even to speak of her brother's perfidious streak, of her twin's treachery toward a most loyal friend.

"How are you?" she asked him timidly instead. She was thinking of when her twin had tried to kill Zac and how he'd coped with his gunshot wounds' treatment afterward.

Zac understood and smiled at her, reaching out to her olive branch. "Fine, thank you. My arm muscles still need physio-therapy, but they are healing. I'm not in a cast anymore after so long, which is heaven. So, yes, things are looking up," he said reassuringly.

She smiled back, pleased he was doing well again.

But Zac reverted back to the issue in hand. "Erin, this is Goran Marshall. He'll take care of you while you are at the clinic."

The young man stood up and extended his hand to her in greeting with a warm smile. They shook hands. She returned a polite, distracted, brief grin.

"Are you a physician?" she asked.

Goran raised his eyebrows, darting his eyes to the two men and back to her.

"Goran works for us," Finley broke in.

"You have a doctor working for you?" she asked, surprised. Besides, the newcomer looked rather young to be a doctor.

"Goran works in our security firm," Finley repeated.

"Why do you need a doctor in a security firm? Do you have many injuries in the line of duty?" she asked, confused, wondering why they'd hired a doctor to look after her if she was going to Dr. Stewart's clinic anyway.

"I am a bodyguard, Miss Blake." Goran's deep baritone voice, with a suave, silken tone to it, floated in the air and reached her ears as if in a dream, seductively.

She stared at him with a captivated expression, now really seeing him for the first time.

Until then, she had barely noticed him, preoccupied with Zac, Finley, and her own sticky situation. Goran had been at the peripheral of her vision, overlooked, almost hidden, and she had not expected such a spellbinding, masculine tone of voice in this rather tall, muscled, young man. Now that she cared to survey him for an instant, she loved what she saw.

But then his words registered. She studied him, bewildered. His hazel eyes returned her stare with a hint of amusement in them.

"A bodyguard?" Erin shouted, astonished, when she had sufficiently recovered. Her dark, large eyes widened in surprise.

"Yes, Miss Blake," Goran said with the same suaveness. His eyes caressed her face with a small, beguiling smile.

"A bodyguard?" she cried out in a louder, shrill voice. "You don't mean…" She stood up abruptly. "You don't mean you'll stick a guard dog on me, do you? Why? What for?" she shouted in a rush, pacing the room, her eyes darting from Zac to Finley questioningly. Her brow wrinkled as her understanding grew, and her eyes flashed at them in sequence.

Then, she settled a fierce scowl on Goran, who had retaken his seat with a resigned expression on his face that said *here we go!* And she followed it with a haughty glance of mockery at him, an insolent smirk on her lips.

"Erin, dear, you must understand, it is only temporary—" Zac started, but she wouldn't let him finish.

"No way! You are not placing him on me!"

"Not literally, Miss Blake," Goran said frivolously.

They all stared at him warningly, to shut him up.

Erin blushed, directing another glance at him that suggested, *I'll kill you if you do!*

But it nonplussed him. The hint of amusement in his eyes grew instead, which irritated her no end.

She fired at him the one thing she knew would bring him down a peg or two. "No. No way. God, look at him, he needs nursing himself. He is but a boy."

"I am twenty-seven, Miss Blake, hardly a boy," he replied coolly.

Zac frowned at him, raising an eyebrow. Perhaps he was mistaken, and Goran was indeed twenty-seven years old, but somehow he didn't think so. But he said nothing, with the situation volatile as it was.

"Do not speak to me!" she flashed at Goran, with a murderous expression on her face. "Besides, I don't need guarding. I am fine," she whined with contempt, pacing up and down the room.

"Darling, it's only temporary, until you get better. Perhaps a few weeks," Finley said in a soothing tone. They had known each other for half of their lives despite their tribulations, so he could speak openly to her.

"A few weeks? No, no way. I am going home! Right now!"

"Erin, please, don't do this. I beg you, we all want the same thing, and you do too. I know. You won't even notice him around you. I promise you," Zac said.

What? Erin thought, astonished.

Good God! Look at him, Goran looks like Michelangelo's bloody David! The difference, he is not a marble statue; he is flesh and blood and hot as hell! How on earth am I not supposed to notice the damn boy?

"No! I've agreed to go to this clinic. Isn't that enough?"

"Please let's not make this more difficult than it is. Let's try it, hey? It's late, and we have an hour's drive ahead of us to the place," Finley replied.

"No, I said!"

Zac's phone rang. He looked at it. "It's the clinic, please excuse us. Finley and I need to take this. We'll be back in a minute. They are probably wondering where you are." So they left the room.

There was an embarrassing silence between Erin and Goran for a minute when they left. She sat back on the sofa and fidgeted with her hands. Then, she raised her head to glance at him. "They think I am going to escape from the clinic, don't they? That I'll do this again. They don't trust me, is that it? Not one bit!"

He looked at her, and she saw a fleeting flash in his eyes. She thought it was compassion, she couldn't be sure. It was followed by a tender glance, then a genuine sweet smile appeared on his face. But it didn't last long. He opened a brief-case on the small table. He rummaged through a file and took something out.

"You scared Miss Kathryn out of her wits, Miss Blake. She was distressed for days. Look at these pictures. This is her, after your brother attacked her in Antibes," he said calmly, polite, but the steely note of coldness in his voice was new and made it even more chilling for her.

Not to mention the horrendous photos of a battered, black and blue Kathryn propped in front of her then. If he wouldn't have told her, she would not have recognized the girl in the pictures. And Erin's brother had done that! Now she, his twin, had been on the verge of a similar path. She closed her eyes and cursed silently. She shivered and looked at Goran with pleading eyes. He removed the photos and placed them back in the folder.

"They'll trust you in time, but you must show them they can. For now, they are not taking any chances. They won't place the girls in danger, and can you blame them?" Goran's voice returned to his velvety tone, but there was a businesslike formality, a self-assurance, a great confidence in him. She had not noticed it before. "I can help you with this, Miss Blake," he finished warmly.

She glanced into his eyes, which now seemed to be expectant, waiting for her to respond. "I see," she mumbled after a while, blinking twice. She reflected for a few moments.

"Can you even bodyguard? You look more like twenty-two than twenty-seven," she said in an undertone, to lighten the atmosphere.

"I can do more than that," he replied with a slight move of his head and a wink, and this time his flippant, smug tone was back in force, the line delivered as smooth as velvet.

She snorted, feeling there was an innuendo there somewhere, yet she wasn't sure. She realized he was making fun of her again, following the serious note. She reared her head in a haughty look that said, *if you think I am falling for that, you are foolish!* But she had.

She had been off sex for a long time. The grief at losing her brother, then within months, losing her parents, had been too great. So for eight months, she had not even thought of it. But that night, of all nights, in Zac's sitting room, a little steer down below between her legs made her clench her buttocks. It was the first time she'd thought of sex; she didn't have much of it either for more than a year prior to that, since she had ended the relationship with her fiancé two years ago.

She was sure her vagina had grown cobwebs, it had been

so long since she'd had any action. A deep sigh escaped her involuntarily. So, at that very moment, and God only knew how, she felt horny and blushed like a teenager.

He must have sensed something in her eyes, and the slow shrill hiss coming out of her mouth caused his lips to curl up on one side.

This made her blush even more.

She rose, ready to leave the room, feeling vulnerable alone with him, but Zac and Finley came back in, saving her from further embarrassment.

"Erin, can we go now? Please. It's late, and the clinic is pressing us to get there," Finley asked, expecting another battle with her on this issue.

But she grabbed her bag and stood waiting for them. When no one moved, astonished she had suddenly agreed, she said, "Well? Are we going or not?"

The girls took refuge in the kitchen when they left the room. With the cook safely tucked up in bed, Mollie hinted at a chair at the table for her friend, while she rummaged in the fridge.

They settled on a slice of apple pie with custard. She warmed it in the microwave. The sweetness of the warm pie restored them to calm, and it was much required after the upheaval of the night.

"By God, I upset my husband," she stressed while she put a piece of pie in her mouth.

"Jesus, he looked furious. Do you think Finley is this cross too? God, your cook is a saint; this apple pie is awesome. I needed this! It is delicious and baked to perfection," Kathryn said as she stuffed another piece in her mouth, too.

"Well, judging by how Fin wrestled me when you went up to Erin's house, I would say yes. He is not happy, though he might have mellowed out by the excellent result with Erin. Zac missed all of that, instead, having to wait at home, alone, not knowing what was going on. I am sure it only made his temper flare more. Are you staying tonight? It is so late to be walking home to yours."

"Yes, I don't think I can move anyway. I'll probably fall asleep right here on this chair."

"Don't be silly; finish your apple pie and go to your room. Have a good night's sleep. Finley won't be back soon. By the time he delivers Erin to the clinic and comes back, it's going to be early morning. Even if he wanted to, poor man, you won't see him until tomorrow now. You'll be safe for tonight." Mollie scoffed, "I'll do the same. I am bushed; I am going to bed. It's almost one am, anyway."

"My room?"

"You know I'll always have a room for you here. But lately, you seem to spend most of your time with Finley. As it should be, mind you. At least, he is making up for the lost time, the cheapskate," Mollie snorted.

"Oh, Mollie, stop that! You know he is generous," she said, which made Mollie chuckle even more.

Chapter 13

Over an hour later, Zac entered the dark bedroom. His gorgeous eyes, the color of mellow cognac, squinted, adapting slowly to the blackness. He stood still under the doorframe, listening, and he closed the door quietly behind himself.

As he moved farther into the room, his sight adjusted to the shadows, and he recognized the familiar shape of Mollie's body in bed. He tilted his head to one side for a few seconds, watching her, wrinkling his brow. Then he paused by the purple velvet ottoman at the foot of the bed, took off his shoes, trousers, and shirt, remaining in his boxers with his tall, fit and toned body well on show.

There was no movement from her.

He observed her for a few more moments, and a smirk played on his face. "I know you are not asleep," he said, his tone firm but with a hint of amusement.

She had no reply, not a sound. She didn't even stir from her position.

"There's no point, Mollie; you are only pretending to sleep.

It's no use. Trust me," he added, letting out a massive sigh, still somewhat amused at his troublesome wife.

He had no reply this time, either.

With long strides, he moved to his side of the bed. She was lying on her flank, with her back to him. He pulled the coverlet all the way down, exposing Mollie's delicate frame in dainty, skimpy shorts and a camisole. He leaned over and smacked her backside once, hard.

That forced her to rise, and she sprang into a sitting position, confronting him. "Bloody hell, Zac, that hurt! How do you do this? How did you know I wasn't asleep, I mean?"

"Your breathing—"

"Umm, ah?"

"Never mind that," he said, turning on the lamplight on his bedside table to illuminate the room. He could see her clearly now. Their eyes locked. He breathed out another sigh of frustration and there was a steely glint in his sultry honey eyes.

She bit her bottom lip in apprehension and gave him a sheepish glance. "I-I—" she stammered.

"What I want to know is who on earth gave you permission to touch my gun, hey? Let alone take it from its case, and with you in that ridiculous expedition of yours. What the hell did you intend to do with it? You foolish girl, are you mad? You could have hurt someone. Guns are not toys; do you hear me? They are dangerous, and most times, they lead only one way. You had no business taking it," he growled. His long lashes blinked in a scowl, then he glared at her, and his expression flashed fire.

She inhaled sharply. Zac looked furious!

He moved closer. He kneeled next to her on the bed, and her eyes were big, looking at him. She tried to move away from him to get off the bed, but he reached out and grabbed her wrist, clasping her.

"Oh, no, no, no! You are not going anywhere! Not so bold now, are you?" He stared at her.

She swallowed. Even in that perilous situation, she glanced at him from head to toe. No use denying it, it never ceased to amaze her. He was the most handsome man she had ever seen, and he was all hers. Even in his irritation, he aroused her. She adored her husband. He looked divine, almost naked but for his boxers, his chiseled, muscular torso as hard as a rock, his wide shoulders that narrowed at the waist so sexy, his thighs powered by incredibly lean muscle. He was gorgeous, and she licked her lips.

At that precise moment, her adored husband was not a cheerful man, though, and she had caused his unhappiness.

She wasn't sure whether to lust after him or dread him. So, she just shrugged her shoulders, not knowing what to say to him, averting his eyes. There was nothing she could say to justify herself, she knew.

With a slick movement, to her surprise, he turned her face down on the bed, and smacked her bottom.

"Ow, ow! It hurts. And why didn't you tell me it was Erin! Ha? You knew!" she shrieked.

"You have no right to any questions after what you did." He pulled her skimpy, pink pajama shorts down to her knees in one go, with her underwear. *Wait!*

"Are you wearing lace knickers? Not cotton?" he asked with an amused smile, noticing her enticingly sexy, little black lace number. He covered her bottom once more with the intricate, black lace panties to admire them, but it didn't stop him from whacking her backside hard over them.

"Ow, ow, please, stop. I thought it might soften you seeing me in lace." She started fighting him, struggling to liberate herself from his clasp. He gave her two powerful smacks that brought tears to the corner of her eyes. Her buttocks were stinging. She wriggled some more, seeking to protect her butt with her hands.

He took her wrists in one hand, pressing them gently but firmly on the small of her back. This had the effect of stopping her wriggling too much, fighting him, thus he held her to the bed solidly.

She swore at him when she could not move anymore; he raised an elegant brow.

"You ape! Stop this, you bear!" she cried out. "I thought you'd like the lace."

"I adore you in anything, Mollie, you know that. I am flattered that you went for black lace to please me; lovely and sexy they are, too," he replied with a satisfied, proud grin, giving a sensuous caress to her saucy backside covered by the splendid lacy number. "But nothing you say or do tonight will save your butt from a good thrashing. You put yourself in grave danger. No one knew how Erin would react. You are a foolish girl, and you don't even realize it. I was worried sick! And with a gun? God, give me strength!" He pulled her panties down to her knees where her shorts awaited them. He raised his hand high and whacked the enticing half-round globes of peachy, creamy skin that formed those perfect buttocks with all his might.

She yelled curses at him with tears in her eyes.

He stopped his big palm on her butt cheeks, warming them, massaging them slowly, after the impact of the sting. The flaming redness matched her hair.

She stilled during his massage, taking a breath. Though it hurt like hell, she enjoyed his hands on her fiery scarlet bottom, and her insides warmed delightfully.

He smacked her hard again, the flesh of her buttocks resonating in the room at the impact of his palm on her skin.

"Ouch, please stop this, now. We'll wake the entire household," she gasped in shock, but her voice sounded midway between a moan and a groan. She was warming pleasurably to the spanking in contrast to her remonstrations. Butterflies danced in anticipation at her core, the heat between her legs spreading fast. Suddenly, it made her wanton despite the suffering, the sting, pain and delight mingling deliciously.

He spanked her with several eye-watering, powerful smacks, at timely intervals. Some landed on the crest of her butt cheeks and others on the crease between her buttocks and legs, at the very tops of her thighs. She pleaded and begged him to release her, with her eyes stinging with tears, but on the inside, a rush of mind-blowing desire flashed through her frame from the tip of her head to her curling toes, and she moaned, arching her backside with pleasure.

"They'll say well done! I can guarantee you that. You made cook almost cry with anxiety. The poor woman was so upset. Mrs. Merton became a nuisance, asking me every few minutes if you were all right. Not to mention, I was almost out of my mind. Just by flipping chance, Finley intercepted you both. Otherwise, God knows what might have happened." And more blows landed in the center of her butt, within her crease, which rendered her speechless with thrill and unbearable suffering.

Her rump was on fire! Nonetheless, it made her arch her derriere to him, exposing it more, offering herself to him. The delight mingling with the pain and the sting, desire spread across her frame, through every pore, each muscle in her body tingling with titillation.

He paused and massaged her backside. His manhood throbbed, too, seeing her flawless butt arched to him, her legs opened slightly, her offer to him. His breath hitched. He stopped for a moment to dispense of his boxers with his free hand, which was not a mean feat in the position they were in.

She turned to him, even in pain. She couldn't help but gaze at his powerful, naked body for a few seconds, his beautiful, sculpted torso, a harmonious ensemble of the finest caliber of manhood she had ever seen, and he was her husband. She licked her lips, despite the burning backside.

More whacks came down on her butt. "Do not ever do that again! Understood!" Two more smacks crashed on her backside. "Answer me!"

His longish, strawberry blond hair came down over his eye and face with the effort of spanking her. He resembled a Roman god venting his wrath on a mere mortal. Despite her arousal, images of the beautiful statue of *Mars Restrained by Cupid*, she had once seen at Chatsworth House in Derbyshire, came to mind. She couldn't help idolizing him, that's how much she loved him, and she longed for her husband to be inside her. In that instant, Zac was flesh and blood pulsating in all his lively splendor, and he was the love of her life.

"Yes, I promise, please, stop!" she cried out, her backside scarlet and incandescent. Despite the pain, she let out a heavy sigh for him. She wanted him. Though her backside hurt with all those whacks, she wished for him to fuck her hard. *God, humiliation!*

He still held her wrists behind her back. She peeked at him, moaning at the sight of him, even with tears in her eyes. While she quivered in the spanking's aftermath, her legs unconsciously parted some more, exposing her slit to him.

He smirked with delight. "Are you going to apologize for upsetting me?" He rubbed her butt again softly, caressing it. As he looked at her red, silky skin in his hand and her exposed sex, his cock throbbed.

"I am sorry. I am!" she whined, but her insides were flipping with bliss at his massage.

"Good! Do you promise never to touch my gun again?" He massaged some more, then two more resonant smacks landed between her bottom cheeks.

"Ahh, ow, ow. Yes, I promise. Please," she cried out with tears streaming, but she moaned, too, in pleasure between cries, somehow voicing her need and arousal to him with her sounds. He moved her hair away and kissed the hollow of her neck.

A thrill rushed through her. Between the kissing on her neck, the stinging of her butt and the massage of it, he was giving her incredible sensations. As he did so, her pussy oozed a trickle that ran through the side of her thigh. Her arousal was phenomenal, and she moaned again.

Each fragment of her body seemed inebriated, intoxicated by desire, waiting for release, while his hand warmed her butt in pure delight. Pleasure flowed like a rushing wind and swept wide within her frame, reaching every nook and cranny of her with intense ecstasy.

"Zac, please, please," she pleaded her need. She demanded him inside her with a vengeance; her pussy throbbed with heat, and his cock alone could soothe that fire.

But he was not in a rush. After all, this was supposed to be a lesson to her. So, he raised his hand again, as if he were to swing a golf shot, soaring from high above his head, and landed six more whacks on her butt, spacing them between the crest of her cheeks, the middle of her ass, and the top of her thighs.

She wailed in shock and moaned in pleasure, lifting her backside another notch, exposing more of her sex to him, now in full view. How much longer would she be able to endure this? Despite the intolerable pain, she was close to coming, her behind stinging, her body almost limp with unbelievable bliss.

Alternating the hard smacks with the massage of her buttocks, he said, "I hope this is a lesson and not only for your enjoyment, hmm… I wonder…" he said, in a way satisfied he had aroused his woman so much.

"Oh, yes, yes, please," she was just able to utter between ragged breaths. Her mind could not focus on anything other than her pleasure.

"I see," he answered. A satisfying smirk spread across his face. His fingers lingered teasingly at her opening, caressing her wet, gleaming slit, playing with it.

She moaned so loud that he replied with a laugh, "Now, who is going to raise the entire household, hey?" He pressed for a second on her clit. More approving moans came out of her mouth, and his cock throbbed again.

His fingertips caressed her entrance, the length of it, a few times teasingly. She held her breath in anticipation. He put a finger inside her, and she purred a slow and contented hiss, then a second finger went in, without moving, teasing her.

"Zac, please..." she whispered and moaned her need in ragged breaths. She needed release.

He withdrew them, and she complained at the loss. Suddenly, he raised her on all fours on her knees, kissing her along the length of her back in sensual little kisses that had her almost losing consciousness at the touch of his lips on her bare skin. While his fingers glided back in moving enchantingly inside her, they spread magic through her frame.

He kneeled behind her while she was in that position and withdrew his fingers against her complaints. He got rid of her shorts and lace panties, then grabbed her ass with his enormous hands and placed his manhood, rock solid, at her entrance. He slammed into her.

She hissed at the fierce ecstasy, every pore in her body stirred and thrilled. Her heart raced thunderously in her ribcage, her pleasure bursting out, and she could not contain herself any longer. A few rough, long strokes was all it took to send her into oblivion, crashing her senses in bliss, her delight prolonged and powerful, her body limp.

He trailed behind a few seconds when his orgasm hit in a long, drawn-out burst. He spilled his seed inside her, thoroughly spent.

Their bodies crashed in a mingle of limbs, heat, and

consumed sex, exhausted. When his senses returned to him, he kissed the skin of her back tenderly. He drew from her and turned, pulling her on top of him, clasping her close, their lips meeting in a satisfying and lingering kiss.

"You are a bloody troublemaker. What am I going to do with you? Hey? Instead of teaching you a lesson, all I do is give you pleasure. That won't do. You might get worse," he teased when they parted from the kiss, his thumb caressing her lips adoringly.

She smiled, spent, unable to even talk. She caressed his beautiful, taut chest, giving him sweet kisses she knew he couldn't resist. It was at moments like this, she wondered how her foolish self had landed such an amazing man. She was the envy of women and men, and he loved her out of all the best people in the world.

He adored the little minx and would forgive her anything. Zac convinced himself she had him wrapped around her little finger, as if he were a teenager with his first girl.

But he would not have her any other way, and they continued their lovemaking frolics several times over that night.

Chapter 14

F inley had driven for over an hour, silently, with Erin in his car, while Goran followed them in his.

She asked him to stop for a restroom break. They stopped at a petrol and bar station along the road. Goran got out of the vehicle to follow her, but one glare from her, and he remained outside and watched her through the glass window while she entered the shop. Finley went around to the back of the store, just in case. It seemed a precaution was in order in the circumstances. They were taking no chances. It ran smoothly. Erin returned to the car, and they continued on their way.

They traveled north to the clinic, deep in the Cotswolds' countryside, toward Worcestershire. It was a dark and cloudy night, with no moonlight. The landscape was pitch-black once they left the motorway.

She was irritated she could not admire the typical English market towns and villages built from honey-colored stone in this part of the country, nor set her eyes on the lovely range of gently rolling hills of outstanding natural beauty. The view would have soothed her. As it was, the darkness only added to her apprehension. It made her feel uneasy.

Perhaps she could have country walks once she was there. *Time off from the clinic? For walks in the countryside? Umm…* Would they let her? Who knew?

She didn't have a clue what to expect from now on. Finley said the doctor would take care of writing her sick note for her work, and the staff there would look after all else, but she didn't pay much attention to him, not caring either way.

It seemed to her, she was following orders like a robot. Perhaps, after a good night's sleep, she would feel like herself and take charge. Though, she wasn't sure she had the energy or spirit to do this, not just yet.

Erin hoped this Doctor Stewart, whoever he was, could help her become herself again, to regain her self-esteem and heal her wounds from the awful feelings that had inhabited her mind in the last few months, to become the level-headed lady she had always been. Not this sorrowful, troubled woman crunched up in this car seat. She sighed, and tears rolled down her face. She was glad it was dark, and Finley couldn't see her like this. It would only embarrass her more.

They were heading toward Broadway, in Worcestershire, a small, charming village, closer to the border with the county of Gloucestershire. She knew they were close, as she spotted the dimly lit shape, in the dark, of the iconic landmark of the Broadway Tower. As they went by, she opened the car window; she needed some fresh air. It was late, and she was tired and starting to doze off. She wanted to keep alert to watch where they were going.

As she leaned her head out, she could smell whooshes of lavender floating in the air, which many farms around the area grew. She inhaled soothingly then closed the window as the chill of night set in.

"How long will I stay here?" she asked suddenly.

Finley spun to her for a moment. "It depends on you, Erin. You need to work with the doctors. You must want to get better and follow their advice. Do as they say," Finley said.

"I see. I am not ill, you know. Not physically, anyway," she replied.

He turned to glance at her, then returned his eyes to the road. "Dr. Stewart runs the clinic. He is a friend, extraordinary talented, and the medical team is first class here. I am sure you'll soon feel at home and comfortable. They'll look after you well. I had a word with him; he knows."

"Knows? Knows what?"

"Well, I-I expect he'll find out by himself, anyway, through talks with you," Finley said.

She flushed. Great job he couldn't see her face, but she knew what he meant. She turned scarlet. He had told the doctor what she had done, her complete history behind it, she assumed.

"And this Goran guy?"

"He is a good man. He'll watch over you, look after you. If you require anything, just ask him. I am not sure if Dr. Stewart allows phones in his clinic and things like that. I hear he is rather strict. If he doesn't, and you need to tell me something, do it through Goran. The doctor knows why he is here with you, and he'll keep his."

"Ahh!"

At one point, they took a turn onto a side road. She had hardly spotted it, and they went deeper into the countryside. The occasional farm lights they had seen up until then disappeared altogether. The night was pitch-black, the moon covered by season clouds hidden in the sky. She could see no lights anywhere in the open landscape, other than the car's headlights on the road. Darkness enveloped them completely. It felt eerie, and Erin was getting more nervous.

Another turn onto a narrow, long lane, soon brought the

car to coast along a high, old limestone wall. They drove for about ten minutes on this lane, when high black iron gates appeared toward the end. The place looked secluded, isolated, and judging by their position, she thought the vast countryside surrounded it.

I guess this is where the rich and famous come to lick their wounds, she contemplated, *out of prying eyes.*

Zac said he would pay for her stay and treatment at the clinic. At first, she had dismissed him and refused, but when he told her the cost, she nearly fainted. She intimated another clinic, more affordable. He wouldn't hear of it. He was set on it. Zac determined she should have the best, which, in the circumstances, melted her heart. So, she changed her mind as she had no alternative but to let him deal with the expense. It was way out of her price range. She wondered if it was worth it.

She couldn't see anything as the car stopped in front of the gates. Her eyes were trying to adjust to the darkness. There was no sign on it anywhere.

She pulled the lapels of her coat closer around her neck; she shivered, but despite the chilly night, her palms were sweaty.

She was glad now Goran would be with her. She wasn't sure if it was the dark night, the isolated place, the high wall, the gates or whatever it was, but it felt creepy to her. She turned her head backwards to glimpse at him. The young man's vehicle had stopped behind them. She took a deep breath, relief washing over her.

Finley got out of the car and stepped toward something alongside the entrance. She realized he was speaking to the security cameras. The gates opened, he returned to the car, and they drove in. Goran came in after them.

They followed the long driveway for about five minutes, with high hedgerow plants on either side of the drive, until they reached a huge square where a magnificent house surrounded by pristine lawns stood tall and stately, towering over the landscape. The ground floor of the house was lit up in places. She glanced out the window, and was surprised, as the vehicle's headlights beamed on it, she saw a delightful Tudor manor with huge cased windows. Impressive, striking and somewhat intimidating. It didn't look like a clinic at all, but a grand country estate. She realized now why it was so expensive. She felt she had gone back in time, to Elizabethan Tudor times. But her spirits rose, and she gave a sigh of relief. At least, the place looked beautiful; she was relieved.

They climbed the few stone steps to the entrance. An old nurse opened the huge walnut doors to greet them. She was in a starchy, light blue, pristine uniform and a white cap, and despite the welcoming smile, Erin could detect the no-nonsense attitude of the woman a mile off.

Everything went on like clockwork. Within twenty minutes, they had filled in forms, signed papers, and rooms were assigned.

It was time for Finley to leave. "I must go," he said. "Be good, and follow the doctors' advice. They only have your best interest at heart. Do you understand? Goran will stay with you for as long as needed."

She nodded moodily, like a child to a parent who is about to drop her at the doors of a boarding school, too upset and scared even to cry out. She was glad now the young man would remain with her.

"Look after her," Finley continued, looking for a moment at the lad, then turning to her again, he added, "anything you want, he'll get it for you, or ask him to contact me if you need me."

She nodded. He kissed her forehead, shook hands with Goran, giving him a quick nod and a warning look before he left, urging the young man to be vigilant, without words, and to take care of her.

She didn't miss the peculiar glance he had given the lad.

It took her all of about ten minutes to settle into her new room. The place was rectangular, with a large window, looking out onto a lawn, but the window had thin bars on it. *Sigh!* It was a good size, rather spartan but comfortable, impeccably clean, with everything she might need.

Though she thanked God, she had the foreboding she would need a drink when she got there, and she was gasping for one. Thinking it unlikely to find a drink cabinet in her clinic's bedroom or that the nursing staff would offer her one, Erin had asked Finley for a restroom stop on the way there. While there, luckily, she had met a girl in the toilets and had the idea to bribe her furtively so she could buy two bottles of wine for her. When the girl brought them back to her, Erin had hidden the bottles under her coat, in two large pockets on the inside, hoping for the best.

So now, she thanked her lucky star for her foresight. She fished out the bottles and put one away, hiding it in her underwear drawer under her smalls, and opened the other. In the absence of a corkscrew, Erin pushed the cork into the bottle. Long years at boarding school had equipped her with little useful skills and aptitudes she was sure would now come in handy in a place like this. She poured the white wine into a cup sitting on the tea and kettle service tray on her desk, and she drank it in one go. *God, I needed the damn drink!*

She was having second thoughts about being there, about the entire debacle, about having agreed to be in this clinic. A big heaving sigh left her lungs. She got herself another cup of wine, when there was a knock at the door.

"Come in," she replied, but not before she hid the bottle of wine in a cupboard and the cup under her bed.

Goran came in. He stopped just past the doorframe.

"I saw the light on, wanted to ensure you were all right," he said with his velvety cadence, darting a swift look around her room, taking everything in.

"Yes, thank you, I am fine." She fidgeted with her hands and peeked under the bed cautiously and at the cupboard, for an instant, and then back at him.

He smiled and stared at her. "Are you drinking, Miss Blake?"

"What?" she mumbled, flushing as red as a tomato, not expecting this question. *Damn!*

"You heard me. Yes, drinking!"

"Well, I-I just had water," she blabbered in consternation. *How on earth did he know?*

He walked straight to her bed and grabbed the cup out from underneath. He smelled the contents. "No. I mean, this drinking! Let's see, where is it? Hey?" he replied with disapproval in his tone and an expression that said, *you are in trouble!*

She crossed her arms over her chest and scowled. He smirked, darting an eye around. He moved to the cupboard, opened it, and fished out the bottle, too. It wasn't difficult when the hiding places were limited.

"Naughty, aren't you?" he said in a too familiar tone. "I knew you had!" He grinned at her.

Fortunately, the second bottle was hidden. *As long as he doesn't open my drawers,* she thought. She went to him, grabbed the bottle and cup from his hand, giving him a contemptuous glance. "Get out of my room," she said, turning her back on him.

He sighed, unflappable. "Have you not read the rules behind the door, Miss Blake?"

"Rules?"

"Yes, the clinic's rules. No drinking allowed is one of them," he said and pointed at the rules blurb written behind the door. "My duties include helping you follow them."

"Help me? My mother is dead, and you are a very poor substitute, so please leave," she said, turning to him with an imperious look. She gulped some liquid from the cup, too.

His eyes narrowed on her.

At that moment, the matronly nurse appeared at the door. She stared at her, at the bottle of wine, the cup in her hands, and at Goran, in turn. A disapproving glance and a crease in her brow accompanied all of these censuring looks.

"Well, I never!" said the woman. "Miss Blake, you are breaking several rules at once. One, drinking is not permitted anywhere on the premises. Two, you have a man in your room who is not even part of our staff, and three, your lights are still on, way past your bedtime. Dr. Stewart insists on discipline. It is the only way to get well," the woman pontificated. She went to Erin and grabbed the offending items out of her hands. Then the nurse directed a stare at Goran.

"You, sir, have no right to be here. Not now, nor for the duration of Miss Blake's stay with us, whatever the circumstances. This room is off limits to you. You can talk to her in the communal areas. While in this building, Miss Blake is in our care. Please return to your room immediately," she went on to him. "And, miss, you have five minutes to turn the lights off before I come back in shortly to check. Besides, it's way over three am. You'll meet Dr. Stewart at nine sharp in the morning. He doesn't like waiting. And you, out, Mr. Marshall, please."

Goran went out with a swift look of sympathy directed at Erin.

"And lights out, please. I'll be back soon!" The woman closed the door and left.

Erin had had enough, but she didn't desire another rebuke from the bossy matron, so she had a fast shower and was in bed in twelve minutes flat, a record. Not even at boarding school had she been so quick. So, when the nurse came back to peer at her silently, later, the room was in darkness, and seeing her in bed, she retired, satisfied.

When the nurse left, Erin gave a sigh of relief. *God, the woman will be a pain in my backside.* She could sense she would make her life difficult. She turned in her bed and stared at the ceiling. *At least the bed is comfortable,* she sighed.

She was bushed. It had been a long and unpleasant day. Well, lately all she seemed to have were disagreeable, horrid days. She wondered what the hell had possessed her to do this. Why had she agreed? For God's sake, she had not been in this place for more than an hour. It already felt dismal, worse than her boarding school when she was a teenager. And this was telling! *I suppose it's either this or the police. Or worse, if I go on in my destructive path.*

She knew now, for however long it took for her to get better, she was between two fires, with Goran on one side, who seemed to have taken it upon himself to be her new guardian. *The ass, not to mention the whole thing governed by Finley.* And on the other, this damn clinic, and this rules-mongering Dr. Stewart and all his staff. She fancied she would be better off in the hands of the police!

Oh, bloody hell! What was she going to do? She wasn't one to respond well to authority. She never had. Neither she, nor her brother, had been naïve, easy children, and difficult adults for sure. Well, at least she had been the sensible twin. But since Peter died, she seemed to have inherited her twin's mischievous, destructive, unpleasant side. *Was that even possible? Could that be?* Was it her way to keep Peter alive, to adopt his flaws? She turned in bed and beat the pillow.

Could it be possible she was turning into her twin? Could she be as bad as he had been? *Oh, Heaven! This is useless!* She must stay here and hope for the best, hope that this Dr. Stewart could make sense of her wild mind and bring her back from the verge of self-destruction.

Good God! For my sins, this will be Hell on Earth, in more ways than one!

She cried, long and hard.

Chapter 15

By the time Finley entered Oxford, it was four am. He went to his apartment, had about two hours' sleep, a shower, then he packed his bag.

He drove back to Zac's. It was gone seven am when he showed up at his house. The men sat at the breakfast table. Finley was famished and tired. His nostrils dilated at the sniff of bacon. He ate a plate of scrambled eggs, several rushes of bacon and toast with gusto, and followed it with two cups of coffee, oozing aroma.

He briefed his companion on the events of the night with Erin and the clinic. "Kat stayed here last night, right?" he inquired.

"Yes. She is sleeping; Mollie, too. They are still deep in the land of dreams."

"Did you warn Mollie against firearms? Not to touch your handgun again? I don't want to pry between you two, but I seem to be responsible for Erin too, now. That's besides my own reckless little chit, only fair to complete the circle," Finley said, raising his brows, but he could not disguise a grin of amusement.

"Oh, yes. The foolish minx, the troublemaker, she won't be sitting comfortably today, I can tell you that much," Zac scoffed. "But then, this *is* Mollie we are talking about. The trouble with the lovely creature is that she has a mind of her own. Lessons seem to be lost on her. She is my cross to bear! She had a good warning, though. She'll behave for a while," he added with a sonorous laugh.

"I see," Finley snorted. "Did your secretary change my tickets?"

"Yes, poor woman. One of these days, Gladys is going to resign. Either that, or she'll kill me. How could you get the holiday break dates mixed up?"

"Sorry! God, you do drive the poor woman hard; she earns every penny you pay her. My secretary is not so accommodating." Finley laughed. "She is more like a schoolmistress; she runs me with military precision. I wouldn't have survived calling her at two am to change my traveling tickets."

"Well, all done. You'd better buy Gladys a present, though. Hey, not that it's any of my business, but shouldn't you be making a move? You need to be going soon."

"I must get the princess out of bed first, which is not a mean feat if you ask me, then we'll be off. Would you please ask Mrs. Johnson to get the driver ready and have the suitcases in the car?" Finley asked.

"Sure."

"In which room is she? Her usual?"

"Her usual."

"What time is my train?"

"About eleven am, I think, so you'd better get a move on. The tickets just arrived. They are on the small table by the window, but beware of the magic spells that lurk on that train," Zac said with a laugh.

Finley snorted and looked at him dubiously. He rose and walked to the window to get hold of the envelope, and perused the tickets. "Bloody hell, the train leaves at ten-forty-five!" He put the envelope in the pocket of his jacket.

"Oh, yes, well—" Zac replied, but his friend interrupted him.

"First things, first." Finley left the room in a hurry.

He climbed the stairs two at the time and headed to her bedroom. He opened the door gently to peek in. Everything was quiet. He moved in and closed it behind himself. Finley smirked and shook his head, watching her fast asleep. "Hey, sweetie, wake up," he whispered, sitting on the side of the bed next to her.

"Umm..." was the only sound out of her. She shifted on her side with her back to him.

The girl is not a morning person. Not his favorite personality trait, but he overlooked that in her, as there were so many more delightful qualities in her defense. Kathryn was sweet, clever, and so sexy. Finley loved her charming shyness, her humor. These were delightful to him. The pretty, saucy young woman was a ray of sunshine for him.

Not an early riser was, probably, one of the two things he didn't quite like about her. The other, her stubbornness, which brought her, sometimes, to a careless boldness, to a doggedness resolve, no matter what. Like the one that had seized her last night, plunging herself into danger at Erin's home. Though, if he had to be honest, he secretly admired this reckless determination of hers, whether he liked it or not, but he would never admit to it. *Too wild and too dangerous...* But he adored the cheeky, impudent minx. The girl was his soulmate; he was convinced of it.

He studied her for a moment, looking at the length of her sinuous body under the covers with pride and satisfaction. She was all his! A pleased expression broke out on his face, lighting up his green eyes with fire. "Come on, lazy head, up you go," Finley said, his lips brushing her neck.

"Umm…" Kathryn mumbled. She flapped her hand behind her like shooing an insect.

He laughed. *The chit!*

He hadn't forgotten the danger she had put herself in with Erin, nor her lies, nor the fact she had taken his knife, but he needed her awake first. He was in a hurry, though, assuming he would ever manage to get her out of bed.

They had a train to catch. He might have to wait to remind her of his rules until later on in the day—why she should not do that again. But first and foremost, he required her up.

"Come on, darling, wakie-wakie, up you go."

"Oh, Fin, it's not even light yet."

"It's gone half past seven! Get ready," he said. He got up, stepping to the window to open the curtains. The light flooded in.

He glanced at her in bed. From where he stood near the window, the sight of her warmed his soul. *The reckless, adorable girl!* And he loved her. He believed she had stolen his heart the moment she had danced with him at Mollie's wedding.

"But why?" she grumbled when the light filled the room, slightly raising her face from the pillow. "It's Sunday. Mid-term-break is coming up this week. My holiday starts here, and I have no intention to get up just yet. Let me sleep," she mumbled and placed her head on the pillow again.

"Then, I shall go away alone."

"Yes, you do that," she murmured hastily, shifting the other way.

He snorted, expecting this would have moved her into action, but the girl ignored him.

"To London," he added.

"To London?" she squealed and sat up in bed swiftly in one go, like a toy on a spring.

He curled his lips on one side and raised a handsome brow to her. "So, London gets more attention from you than I do? Is that it?" he set forth with a scowl, though there was delight in his eyes.

"Darling, London wins anytime; you know that," she replied with a playful grin.

He came back to the bed and sat next to her. "But who said I am taking you with me? After your abominable behavior last night, hey? I don't think you deserve it!" he declared, moving her long, messy hair back from her face and trailing his fingers on her pretty, rosy cheeks.

She went crimson. "Oh, Fin, I am sorry I lied; I swear I am," she said, pleading and pouting her soft lips to him. "But consider this; it all turned out for the best. You took Erin to the clinic, right? She is there now, isn't she?"

"Correct!"

"She's going to have treatment to get better, isn't she?"

"Yes." He caressed her pretty lips with his fingers.

"Then, all's well that ends well. There you are."

"You mean, the end justifies the means?" he asked as he rose again, standing tall with a hand flap in the air to dismiss her statement.

"Yes, exactly! It was all for a good cause," Kathryn persisted.

He shook his head. *The chit believes doggedly she was in the right to act as she did.*

"No, it doesn't! Not in my book, and not where you are concerned. I forbid this kind of behavior! Do you hear me? You couldn't foresee what might have happened. Erin may have turned violent and injured you. It was reckless. And with a gun and a knife? A jerky action could have fired a shot. Someone could have been hurt!" He stared her down with his hands akimbo, listing all the potential consequences of her rash actions if he had not been there.

"Well, technically, Mollie was the one with a gun. I only had a knife," she mocked him, amused, with a little childish pout as if pretending to ask forgiveness, but a hard stare from him and she closed her mouth abruptly, pressing her lips. It wasn't the moment to make fun of it.

"Madness! Both of you were out of order!" His face had taken on a darker countenance, imagining what could have happened.

"Oh, but it all ended well. Erin will be fine; she is in expert hands now, is she not? And Mollie and I are okay too. No harm done," she replied, and he gave a long drawn-out sigh, and sat back next to her on the bed, rather disheartened at her stubbornness in defending her actions.

"Oh, for God's sake, you are exasperating. No harm done? Get up, get ready, immediately, before I change my mind, or I'll go on my own. I am being too lenient with you today. I don't think you deserve to go anywhere after last night. But we'll deal with this later, there's no time now. Up! Now!" he rebuked her.

She sprang out of bed but nestled between his legs, while he was still sitting. She put her arms around his neck and kissed him with ebullience all over his face. "Forgive me?" she pleaded while her honey, mellow kisses continued to hit his face randomly.

He laughed, placed his hands over her waist, rose again, and took over kissing her ravenously. Holding her hair in his fist gently, his tongue burst into her mouth as they kissed for a while until he pulled his head back.

"No time for this now, either, or to deal with your appalling behavior last night, princess, but you are not off the hook yet, not by a long shot! And only because you kiss this good, I shall take you with me. So off you go, get ready, and hurry, or we'll miss our train. Your bag is packed," he said when they parted from their kisses, looking into her eyes.

"My bag?"

"Yes."

"Packed?"

"Yes."

"But how long are we going for? Who packed my things?" she asked, surprised, thinking they were going to London just for the day.

"Oh, don't worry about that now, just get ready. It's gone eight am; hurry."

She darted down to the dining room for a quick cappuccino when she was ready.

Mollie was at the table with Zac. The ladies kissed each other's cheeks and said their good mornings all around.

"Kat, you must hurry, just have a coffee. You don't have time for breakfast; we'll get some on the way. If you had left bed when I asked you—" Finley rebuked, but he didn't finish his sentence.

"Fin is taking me to London," Kathryn revealed to her companions over her shoulder, cutting him off, then she turned to the sideboard. She brushed his remark off with a shrug. She poured two cups of coffee, sipping one and giving the other to him.

"Oh, really? That's marvelous. I hope you have a good time," Mollie said and launched Finley a sudden wink when Kat wasn't looking, but Zac pressed his wife's hand hard as a warning.

"Ouch!"

"What is it?" Kathryn turned to her.

"Oh, I bit my tongue," the girl replied sheepishly.

Finley finished his coffee in one go. "Ready? We must leave now," he said, looking at his girlfriend. *Before Mollie puts her foot in it.*

"But, darling, my coffee, I only had two sips."

"Say goodbye." He pulled her by the wrist out of her chair and out of the house.

"Have a pleasant trip," their friends launched in unison as they left.

Chapter 16

A car was ready, waiting for them outside.

"Are the suitcases in the back?" he asked the driver as he patted his pockets with tickets and documents.

"Yes, sir." The man nodded.

"Can I see my bag, check that—" Kathryn said, but Finley didn't let her finish. He tapped his forefinger on her lips twice, though gently. It told her in no uncertain terms, with one flash at the car seat and a long hard glance at her, to get in. He stared her down in that one look that chastised her and aroused her but, at that moment, also suggested, *I am running out of patience.*

She jerked into motion into the seat without another word, but crossed her arms over her chest with a pout.

"God, you can be weary, love! Sometimes, I think you are a child in a woman's body. I told you, we'll miss the fucking train. It's eight-forty-five already; the traffic will hit us," he complained as he sat next to her in the back seat and asked the driver to go, fast.

"Jesus, Fin. Oxford station is ten minutes away from here.

We could have walked," she said, but he didn't answer. When they passed the station and continued on toward the motorway to London, she turned her questioning eyes to him.

"We are not going to Oxford station," he mumbled.

"Where, then?" she asked with her almond shaped, chestnut eyes big and incredulous.

He smiled at her without a word and winked. His green eyes lit up instead. His annoyance was forgotten, and the surprise he had prepared for her rekindled his delight at her company.

She peered out the window at the signs as they went by, then at him, perplexed. "Where are we going? I thought we had a train to catch?"

"And we do."

"But we are traveling toward London."

"We are!"

"In the car, though."

"Well done, Sherlock."

"Where the deuce are we going to get this train?"

"You must wait. Be patient, won't you? And mind your own business until then." He chuckled.

"But if we are going to London to catch a train, where the hell are we traveling to? London is not our final destination then?"

"Oh, my clever little minx is finally awakening. But I am saying nothing." He grabbed her face with his enormous hands and gave her a big, wet kiss, his tongue in command.

"Oh, Fin!" She pouted with a frown when they stopped the kiss. "Why won't you tell me, hey? You do realize Mother gets anxious, since Father died two years ago. She gets nervous about these things, if she doesn't know where I am," she said, a little worried herself, but using different tactics to get to what she wanted to know.

He smiled. "Don't worry, love. Mollie will take care of your mom. But only when we are on the train," he replied and leaned over to kiss the tip of her nose and her forehead.

"Mollie knows where we are going? And she didn't tell me?"

"I didn't tell her; she is supposed to know only after we board the train, so she'll phone your mother then. But it won't surprise me if she already does."

"Why can't I phone my mother myself after we board the train?"

"Well, you must wait and see."

"Oh, Fin. I can't bear not knowing… surprises always make me nervous," she said, dismissing him. "Besides, if Mother realizes I am going away with you for a few days, she may demand you marry me immediately," she taunted him, and he gave her a sidelong glance, but he said nothing.

She flushed at her unwitting remark, when she realized what she'd said. She felt embarrassed at her foolish words. *Jesus, I've put my foot in it! Dear God! We have not been together two weeks yet, and he'll think I already want to marry him. Well, if truth be said… silly girl, stop that!*

He laughed, caressed her hair back behind her ear, and kissed her forehead.

As the journey progressed, they entered London, through Paddington, and they continued along the wide, elegant Bayswater Road.

She looked out the window. Kathryn had been to London several times through the years. But she wasn't sure of the roads by car, though she recognized where she was as they drove alongside Hyde Park on the Bayswater Road, full of the Sunday morning joggers in flow.

She directed a gigantic smile at him. He ruffled her hair. Then, they rounded into Park Lane, down all along until they reached Piccadilly. Her eyes grew big and round, looking at everything. She was in complete awe, directing sweet, brief smiles at him, like a child in a candy shop, while he grinned like a Cheshire cat, proud at her delight. Then, they turned left to Grosvenor Square and finally to their destination, in London's Victoria Station where the car stopped.

He got out of the vehicle and offered his hand to her. She took it, darting a look around with that pretty face of hers, her huge, brown doe-eyes in ecstasy, and his heart almost melted for her.

She had been to this station once, to catch a train. Kathryn was dumbfounded and didn't know what to think.

The driver deposited the bags on the floor. Finley picked them up, thanking the man.

"Are we going for a few days to Brighton?" she asked him excitedly, knowing Victoria Station took people to all the wonderful places on the South Coast of England.

He looked at her with a smile and winked. "Come; move on, hurry! It's almost ten am!" He carried the bags with a firm, speedy step into the station. She accompanied him at the trot, trying to catch up to his purposeful, fast strides, but his walk turned into a military march. The force of habit, in certain circumstances, died hard, the ex-army captain taking over command, hurrying her along, leading maneuvers.

She followed him at a pace. "Fin, slow down, please," she said as they marched with military precision through the busy, crowded London Victoria Station, full of Sunday trippers.

He either didn't hear or ignored her, as he turned over his shoulder, directing a quick movement of the head at her that said *hurry!* And she stepped up her speed.

Finally, he stopped on platform two, outside an office. She stopped behind him, looked up, reading the elegant sign on the office's door.

"The Orient Express?" she said in a gasp.

He directed the most mischievous glance at her, marveling

with delight at her big eyes, almost out of orbit by now. He chuckled.

"But I'll need a passport, won't I?" she added, rapidly recovering after a few seconds, knowing this train would take them out of England. Not that she had ever been on it, but she could read the various destinations along the route on the board.

"Yes, you do!"

"But I don't have it. You should have told me. Where are we going?"

"Come on, love, move. In we go. I've got it."

"You have my passport?"

"Yes, hurry; let's go in. We need to check-in," he said. When she didn't move, dumbfounded, he said, "Move, now, woman!" He shouted it like a military command. She went in after him at a pace.

Finley checked them in. The office gave them their seat allocations for the train from London to Folkestone. Then they were given their sleeping-car compartment number for the Continental train. This second train, on the other side of the English Channel, would take them from Calais, in France, and then forward through continental Europe.

He checked-in their luggage through to Calais, which would wait for them in their sleeper carriage when they boarded the continental train.

The beautiful train of restored 1920s and 1930s British Pullman cars soon rolled in, hissing and puffing, onto the platform.

For a moment, she stood there, dumbstruck, then she glanced at him next to her, the most handsome man, to her, the sweetest of human beings, and if she had not been in the middle of the busy Victoria Station, she would have kissed him long, hard and wantonly. As it was, furtively, she only blew him a kiss. He laughed, recognizing what she wanted to say. Sometimes words were unnecessary between them.

They boarded the train, and a steward took them to their seat.

Kathryn's eyes were enormous with wonder. She followed him like a puppy, in shock at that point. It wasn't just the moment; she was in awe of him, of Finley, of his caring temperament, his tender nature, his attentiveness to her, and even in his bossiness, he made her feel important to him. He had thought of everything, packing her bags, picking up her passport...

She always had to work hard for the things she wanted. No one had ever surprised her with anything, let alone something so lovely. And suddenly, her love for this wonderful man swelled in her heart exponentially. It skyrocketed to the infinite universe and back, with no boundaries or confinement. It poured out of her. The man had brought her existence upside down, fabulously, the fellow she had fallen in love with over eight months ago, and now he was hers. And she was most definitely his, forever. He was her man! Her own clever, affectionate, sexy, handsome man, and sometimes, her authoritarian bad boy. But she wouldn't have him any other way.

They were seated in the plush armchairs, in an open-plan saloon, arranged as intimate tables. Finley had requested a table for four, with more privacy and space, all by themselves.

Shortly after they sat, they were off.

"Well, we made it! Just in time," he said with a satisfied grin, giving her a peck on the cheek while sitting next to her.

"Oh, my word! Fin, the Orient Express! Where are we going, Paris, Innsbruck, Verona? To Venice, where, where?" she shouted the last few words, then she trailed off her voice, embarrassed.

"Oh, quiet, woman, you ask too many questions," he said with a smirk.

"I must admit, I'm shocked. You led me to believe we were traveling to Brighton," she smirked. "Don't get me wrong; there is nothing amiss with Brighton. I would have enjoyed it so much. But the Orient Express! I can't believe I am sitting here. May I explore a bit? May I have a look around?" she asked with a smile that had not left her face since they arrived on the platform.

He laughed. "Be my guest."

Ten minutes later, she returned to her seat, full of excitement. "Oh, this is marvelous!"

"Well, my love, kiss me and make it good," he said, but she slapped his arm in consternation.

"Fin! They'll think we are ruffians," she said with a breezy laugh, but she kissed him anyway, hard and fast, to his great delight.

When the train left Victoria Station, it hissed across the River Thames. It passed by the Battersea Power Station, taking its course toward Folkestone, where they would cross the English Channel to reach continental Europe.

The train went the long way around, via Canterbury and Dover, dropping off day-trippers at Canterbury, and then doubling back along the scenic coastal route to Folkestone.

A three-course brunch was served on the way, which Kathryn ate with gusto, having missed breakfast, and she accompanied the brunch with a sparkling Bellini cocktail.

They seemed to have entered the roaring 1920s, with the decor, the exquisite elegance, and the impeccable service.

But when she ordered her third Bellini, Finley raised an eyebrow, grabbed the drink from the waiter who was about to give it her, and shook his head disapprovingly at her. "No more," he said.

She grimaced. "Oh, Fin, they are so delicious."

"Two Bellinis are more than enough for you. I want you

sober later on, my love. Very sober for what I have in mind."
He whispered the last two sentences in her ear.

She blushed furiously and snorted.

This part of the journey ended in Folkestone East. After a
brief rest stop, which enabled them to stretch their legs in the
terminal, they crossed the sea, the Channel, somewhat spuri-
ously on board of a car-carrying Euro tunnel shuttle train.
They went through the underwater tunnel below the sea bed
that ran beneath the English Channel, to emerge at the other
end in Calais, France, in continental Europe.

The trip from London Victoria to Folkestone had only whet
her appetite for the Orient Express, giving Kathryn a small
glimpse of what was to come, and it could only be compared
to a delicious appetizer of a gourmet dinner, as she now
prepared for the mouth-watering main course.

At Calais, they boarded the first class, fabulous Orient
Express continental train of restored blue-and-gold 1920s
wagons-lits sleeping-cars, bound for Paris, Innsbruck, Verona
and Venice.

The smart stewards in full pristine uniforms welcomed
them on board.

It was almost five pm by the time they were shown to their
carriage, where Kathryn almost wet her pants when she was
surrounded by the splendor of the wagons, a brilliance of
grand style.

Kathryn darted her eyes everywhere, touching everything
as if she were a child, smiling at everyone, launching little
marvelous, loving glimpses at him like she would at a god from
Olympus.

Finley made fun of her enormous eyes, but she never
stopped directing those cute brief smiles at him, full of grati-
tude, awe and love.

He felt it palpably too, more than he cared to admit.

Finley loved the saucy minx, and some raw, powerful

emotion, over and above, stirred in his soul. He was pensive. He wasn't sure if he had succumbed to the atmosphere too.

The train sleeping-car was a classic 1929-vintage wagon-lit. It was composed of two berth compartments that transformed to a private sitting room, with a sofa and a small table for daytime use. When they got to their compartment, it was laid out to daylight use and inlaid with exquisite woodwork every-where, with decorative patterns. It was so highly polished, she could see her own reflections in every panel.

Kathryn had to pinch herself, when she realized she was going to travel, even if she didn't know her ultimate destination yet, in one of the most luxurious sleeping-cars ever built.

She was full of emotion, her hands caressing the intricate panels. While he looked on at her, she directed little tender smiles at him. She took her coat off and perched it on a hook.

He wanted to take her into his arms and kiss her senseless, but he knew she was enjoying herself, looking at everything, exploring, touching and feeling it all, as if she were a baby in her first crawling steps.

She patted the large sofa, convertible to an upper and lower berth at night, with a dainty footstool and a small, elegant folding table. Kathryn opened a beautiful wooden door by the large window to reveal a washstand with soap, towels, flannels and other paraphernalia. She caressed the soft pure cotton white dressing gown. She took her boots off and put on the squashy slippers provided. She passed a pair to him, too.

He laughed, closing the door to the washstand.

She stood there for a moment and looked at him. Then, she flung her arms around his neck tightly. "Oh, if I adored you before, now I-I—" she murmured, but she couldn't finish as he brought his lips to hers.

He drew the blinds down as he kissed her, without breaking the hold on her lips, thus the train rolled out, hissing and chaffing out of Calais Station, and ventured into the heart of Europe.

He pulled her down with him on the large sofa and kissed her hungrily until a knock on the door made them both jump out of their skin.

She sat up quickly, and Finley, too. She smoothed her hair and skirt with her hands.

"Come in," he said, after having darted a look at her, ensuring she was composed.

She flushed crimson, anyhow, when the Maître d' came in, handing out dinner reservations, and she didn't even know why.

Finley made a quick calculation. He wanted time alone with her.

"I would go for the late sitting for dinner. Is it fine for you?" Finley asked her. She nodded, not sure what dinner arrangements she was agreeing to, but if it was cool for him, it was great for her.

The man left.

Finley locked the door this time; he wasn't taking any chances, and they resumed where they had left off. They kissed, his tongue bursting into her mouth, sparring with hers, owning hers hungrily. Their souls responded to the amorous emotions. They didn't stop, as if they were teenagers on their first crush.

He unbuttoned her blouse, and his lips circled her nipple. He began to suck the pink tip deeply and lightly bit it; alternating nipples, he sucked greedily until her panties soaked and her nipples were tuned purple, pert and hard.

Suddenly, he stopped. Then, he rose. She looked at him, bewildered. He grinned mischievously. He pulled her up from the seat too, then he sat down on the sofa again, comfortably. But this time, with a firm pull, he brought her face down over his knees, lifted her skirt to her waist and pulled her panties down to her knees.

"What are you d-doing?" she stammered. Still thoroughly dazed from his kisses, for a moment, she didn't realize he was going to spank her.

"First things first. Now, my love, your punishment is well overdue, or do you think I had forgotten your appalling behavior from last night, hmm? I must not indulge you too much, or you'll wrap me around your little finger."

"But, Fin, why?" she mumbled. "We talked about it." She continued to complain, but he whacked her bottom solidly, twice on each buttock, leaving red imprints of his digits and palm as her speech halted with his painful whacks.

"Ow, ow, please," she pleaded. The stinging on her backside soared as another set of whacks landed on her butt. Though, with the previous steamy kissing and her nipples well sucked just before the smacks, the spanking only raised her temperature to sizzling levels. Her pussy gleamed with wetness.

She was ready in no time. She needed release. But he smacked her bottom again, right in the middle of her buttocks, and her breath hitched. Then the shift of more smacks at the very top of her legs, repeatedly, made her lose any coherent thoughts. She wasn't sure whether to complain or to will him on, her dichotomy of liking it and hating it was too strong.

"Fin, please, stop! It hurts."

"This reckless streak of yours must cease, understood?" he said, but it was the turn of hard smacks on the crest of her round, beautiful, plump buttock cheeks. He adored her ass! He whacked her gorgeous derriere solidly, the whole of her backside utterly smacked, not an inch of her perfect peachy, creamy skin left untouched by his powerful hand.

She complained. Tears flooded her eyes. The stinging was unbearable, but her pussy wanted more.

"Quiet, my love," he admonished her, "you don't want to be a disturbance on this train, do you?" He whacked her again.

She hissed in pain.

He raised his palm above his head, as if he were about to swing a ball, and smacked her backside. Then he quit, with his hand on her bottom, massaging it.

She stilled, taking a breather but embarrassed at her own thrill for the spanking. If she had to admit it, she was soaked. Kathryn exhaled, and her legs parted as if of their own volition, so brazenly and wantonly, he laughed.

"You are a naughty girl! You know that? In more ways than one."

This invitation only caused the already almighty hard-on of his cock to swell and throb. He touched her slit, caressing it, then slid his fingers inside her.

Her breath hitched.

He teased her folds, then he withdrew.

She moaned, wanting more unashamedly.

"Umm, Kat, you do realize this is supposed to be a punishment, for getting my knife, for the lies, for the appalling behavior of last night? Understood? Not a titillating, teasing sex game as you are taking it to be. Do you hear me?"

"Yes, yes. Please," she mumbled, but she was pleading her need. She was so close; she craved release.

"Not for your enjoyment—"

"No, please, Fin," she pleaded through ragged breaths, but more mighty, powerful whacks made her body shudder with pleasure and pain. She called his name out in short, sweet little cries as he plunged two fingers inside her again, riding her to the crest of her orgasm before he realized or intended.

She almost lost consciousness as she shuddered and shivered in her ecstasy, her body limp and spent with the pleasure.

He pulled her up into his arms, and more ravenous kisses followed. "God, I wonder if that was really a punishment, umm hey? No more reckless behavior. Next time, I won't be so lenient, understood? You naughty minx," he said, pulling his head back, and she gave him a small smile, but soon his lips went back to hers.

They kissed for a while, caressing each other, and she was soon ready for more.

"Did you hear me? You promise? No more bravado?"

"Oh, Fin, yes," she said feebly, and he kissed her again.

Then, he pushed her down on her back gently. He took her panties off, then his jeans, parted her legs and slipped inside her, still both half-dressed.

Her juicy pussy felt amazing as he moved in and out of her repeatedly. He stopped for a second. She clenched her walls against his swollen cock. His manhood throbbed, and he thrust slowly at first. "God, you are so wet, love," he panted between breaths.

"Fin, darling,"

"Oh, God! Kat, I love you," he murmured.

Her senses returned at these, so far, unspoken words. As he moved harder, deeper inside her, there was a renewed fervor between them, a revived passion.

"I love you too, more than you know," she echoed, her chest heaving as she felt every inch of him inside her, riding her, bringing her to the verge again. His passionate declaration of love only made it sweeter for her, elevating her emotions to another level.

He kissed her then plunged into her with the sentiment that she was his soulmate, the woman of his dreams, the only girl for him—his woman!

The same conviction harbored in her soul. He was her man, the love of her life. But soon, her thoughts became inconsequential as she pleaded for release in her typical sweet little cries.

He slammed into her, hard, faster, with his whole body

behind him, wanting more of her, forever. The elegant compartment twirled around her, until the rapturous pleasure reached every nook and cranny of her frame and she shivered in a delirium of love.

"Marry me?" he whispered as he suddenly peaked too and shuddered with all his might inside her. Waves of blissful joy washed over him, over and over. He slumped over her as their emotions subsided, their half-clothed bodies in a tangle in that unusual surrounding.

The train had weaved its magic on him, more than he cared to admit if he had to be honest. But she had long cast her spell on him. The sorceress had bewitched him long ago. The mythical, enchanting atmosphere of the train, working its charms to the fullest, had only spurred him on to a destination he was surely bound to, regardless. She'd had him in the palm of her hand for months, anyhow. And now, he'd said more than he had bargained for, twice over!

She heard the sweet expressions of love from him as she echoed her sentiments back to him, but did she hear him say his whispered words, *"Marry me?"*

If she had, she didn't let on. She just kissed him longingly for some time, but there was no answer to his question.

It astonished him he'd said those words, but he had. He had asked her to marry him! *Good Lord!* Though he didn't regret it. No! But when she made no reply and gave him no hint of having heard his words, he had cold feet thinking she might not want to, that he was running too fast for her. She was still young, anyway. So, he let it drop.

He was too happy, in the moment, to rock the boat. So he pretended he didn't say a word. In any case, it seemed she hadn't heard them, anyway.

Nonetheless, he wasn't sure if he was relieved or upset.

They dressed in their finery for dinner as the train was about to arrive in Paris. But when he didn't move to pick up the luggage or hurry, and they still had supper to look forward to on the train, she turned to him. "It's not Paris then?" she inquired with a smile.

"Not Paris!" He smiled back, but she didn't ask where they were going like she had done many times earlier in the afternoon.

Perhaps she had heard his words, and now he had spoiled the trip by asking that stupid question. *Who on earth asks a woman to marry him after only two weeks? Is that even possible? How could you be such a fool?* he asked himself. In all likelihood, he had scared the girl off, which was exactly what he had tried to avoid all this time. He cursed himself.

He took her hand and kissed her palm, looking at her. She reddened and smiled. He cuddled her into his arms. "You look beautiful. Come on, love; let's go to dinner."

They went out to the restaurant car, to the Etoile du Nord, a magnificent car built in 1929, with its unique decor, elegant and sophisticated.

As dinner commenced, the journey rekindled too, onward from Paris, and the train moved forward through the continent.

She loved the ambience and the romantic supper.

Finley only had eyes for her. He seemed to have zoned in on her, as if the rest weren't there, as if they were alone. He replied to others politely and gentlemanly, but his eyes were only on her. "I really meant it, when I said I love you. I do!" he murmured to her, and she blushed scarlet.

"I love you too, Fin; you know that," she whispered back.

He squeezed her hand over the table. Suddenly, they were like two teenagers, whispering sweet things to each other in the middle of the busy restaurant car, through the huffing and puffing of this striking compartment, amongst spectacular scenery, as the train whooshed and whizzed like a bullet through the beautiful French countryside.

Afterward, they went to the bar-car for drinks, admiring the scenery outside, as a full moon beamed a silver light over the landscape, and relishing each other's amorous company. But soon they returned to the compartment, now converted into a bedroom with the upper and lower berths made up and ready for the night.

She launched herself on the bottom one. "Wow! This is comfy. Which one will you take? I don't mind." She adjusted the pillows under her head.

"The same one you'll take," he replied playfully.

For the rest of the night, he kept his word and stayed in bed with her, making sweet love to her until they were utterly spent and fell asleep in each other arms.

He woke up at first light. For once, she was already up ahead of him, standing, peeking through the blinds out of the window, with her back to him. She turned, hearing him move. Seeing him awake, she smiled at him and pulled the blinds up. The early morning light flooded in the compartment.

The journey had progressed through the night as the train left French soil and rode into a new country. With the new light of day, the magnificent scenery hit her as they rumbled through Switzerland. She had woken up somewhere beyond Zurich, while the train was running southeast alongside the sparkling waters of Lake Zurich, with the breathtaking snowy mountains' peaks of the Swiss Alps as a backdrop.

She looked out the window, mesmerized by the stunning scenery and the grand lake. She turned to glance at him. There was a glint in her eyes, like when someone discovers something wonderful and meaningful, so she turned back to the splendid white peaks and the gleaming waters outside as the train dashed on through.

"Where are we going?" she asked over her shoulder at him. "You can tell me now."

He snorted and passed a hand over his face. "To Venice, in Italy."

"Venice!" she exclaimed, turning to him again with big eyes. A huge grin spread over her pretty face, from ear to ear. "I knew it. I knew it!" she repeated several times.

He laughed and got up from bed, coming to stand next to her by the window to admire the scenery with her.

"Did you mean it last night?" she asked him suddenly.

He side-glanced at her, then he caressed her hair back behind her ear and planted a kiss on top of her head. "Yes, I love you, darling," he said. He gently touched her face as she stared out the window at the snowy Alps and the glistening waters of the grand lake in wonderment.

"God, this is beautiful!" she said in awe at the landscape. She peeked at him and added, "No, I mean the other one." She became scarlet.

"The other one?"

"Yes, the other question!"

"What question?" But he knew what she meant. *So she did hear me!*

"Come on; did you mean it? Do you want to marry me?" she persisted. This time, she spun to him, trying to determine the veracity of his words.

He looked at her, and for a calm and burly man, a flush crept up on his neck. "Yes, I do," he said steadily.

She studied him seriously, suddenly pensive. "Then, bloody go down on your knees, man, and do it properly!" Kathryn declared in all seriousness.

Finley chuckled, stared at her, bewildered for a moment, then he got down on one knee. He looked into her lovely, expectant face. "Oh, bloody hell, I don't have a ring," he mumbled.

"What? No ring?" she uttered, astonished.

"No!"

"But you asked me to marry you."

"I know."

"Without a ring?"

"Yes, but this, darling, wasn't planned. I can assure you," he explained, standing up again. She looked at him, confused, her eyes big. Her hands clasped the side of her robe, unsure of what to do next.

"You mean to say, you brought me on this journey not intending to propose to me?"

"No, not really."

"This is just meant to be a delightful journey for us to enjoy?"

"I am afraid so!"

"You didn't intend to pop the question to me then?" she uttered in a strangled voice.

"Well, not now, no! I-I... Mollie kept saying I am a cheap-skate for not taking you out on a nice date and I—"

"Are you saying we are on the Orient Express because Mollie thought you were a cheapskate?"

"No, love, not Mollie. I didn't want *you* to think it," he explained. Perhaps, for the first time in his life, he felt embarrassed.

"Oh, God, for an authoritative and dictatorial brute, some-times, big man, you can be remarkably absurd!" she replied with a joyous grin.

He lifted an elegant brow, shooting a dubious look at her with a wrinkle in his forehead.

She roared with laughter. "Oh, you silly man! How could you think this of me?"

"I—"

"But you proposed to me! I heard the words, clearly."

"Yes, I know! I did."

"You mean to say you did it on the spur of the moment? Out of the blue?"

"Not out of the blue, Kat. I do love you. I would have done it, anyway, at some point soon, but no, it wasn't planned for this trip. I would have had a ring if I had planned it, girl. Hell, yes, I would. But the words took even me by surprise, though they came from the heart," he added with a nervous laugh, caressing her face.

"Umm, so you don't want to marry me, then?"

"Oh, no. I mean, yes, no, I do! Yes," he blabbered like a teenager.

"Yes or no?"

"Yes, yes! Definitely yes!"

"Are you certain?"

"As sure as night and day! As sure as a man who loves his woman can be!"

"You still want to do it then?"

"Why, yes, if you'll have me," he replied resolutely.

"Then do it, man. Now! On your knees, Finley Harman, and make it good!"

He scoffed.

"Here, use my ring as a token, then you can buy me a proper one," she suggested, offering him her own ring.

He smiled, took her ring and went down on one knee.

"Kat, my love, I am head-over-heels in love with you, and I want to spend the rest of my life with you. Will you marry me?" he asked expectantly.

She gave him her best smile, and with eyes full of love, she replied, "Oh, yes, Mr. H-Harman! I-I will marry you. I-I will." Her voice was full of tiny tremors, while her eyes glistened. She flung her arms around his neck.

He stood, circled her waist, and kissed her lovingly. When they parted from the kiss, he took her hand and put the ring, her own ring, on her finger as a token of their promise.

"You'd better buy me a nice one," she said and snorted.

He caressed her lips with his thumb, in awe of this spirited young woman who had stolen his heart.

Thus, somewhere between Calais, France and Lake Zurich, Switzerland, surrounded by the Alps, on the Orient Express, unwittingly, they found themselves engaged to be married.

The magic had cast its spell, with their hearts bursting out with a love so pure and tender to last them a lifetime.

The End

Raffaella Rowell

Raffaella was born in Italy and grew up in South America. She moved to England in her mid-twenties, where she currently resides. She is married and has two sons.

She has a university degree in Modern Languages and Literature. She loves a book in any genre, reads anything and every day, with a weakness for crime/thrillers, romance novels, classics and historical figures.

Raffaella writes romance novels with a twist of suspense, spicy and sexy in the midst. She also enjoys gardening, baking (legendary for her delicious baked cheesecake), and playing the piano.

Email: raffabellano@gmail.com
Instagram account: @raffaellarowell
Twitter account: @Raffaella Rowell
Visit her website here:
www.raffaellarowell.com

Don't miss these exciting titles by Raffaella Rowell and Blushing Books!

The Perfect Pairing
The Trouble with Mollie
Ice, Spice and Red Lace

Blushing Books

Blushing Books is one of the oldest eBook publishers on the web. We've been running websites that publish spanking and BDSM related romance and erotica since 1999, and we have been selling eBooks since 2003. We hope you'll check out our hundreds of offerings at http://www.blushingbooks.com.

Blushing Books Newsletter

Please join the Blushing Books newsletter
to receive updates & special promotional offers.
You can also join by using your mobile phone:
Just text BLUSHING to 22828.